M000107120

RIDDLED
to DEATH

Books by Joanne Clarey

<u>FICTION</u>
Twisted Truth
The Mysteries of Hummingbird Falls
Skinned (October 2006)

<u>NONFICTION</u>
I. A.M. G.R.E.A.T. (GROWTH THROUGH
RESOCIALIZATION, EXPLORATION, AWARENESS
TRAINING)

I. A.M. P.O.O.W.E.R. (PROMOTING OCCUPATIONAL
OPPORTUNITIES FOR WOMEN THROUGH
EXPERIENCE AND RETRAINING)

To Kent –

Have a good read!

RIDDLED to DEATH

Joanne Clarey
2008

Joanne Clarey

Published by Alabaster Books
North Carolina

This is a work of fiction. Names, character, places, and incidents either are the product of the authors imagination or are used fictitiously and any resemblance to actual persons, businesses, events, or locales is coincidental.

Copyright 2006 by Joanne Clarey
All rights reserved. Printed in the United States of America.
No part of this book may be reproduced in any manner whatsoever without written permission except in the case of brief quotations embodied in critical articles and reviews.

Published by Alabaster Books
P.O. Box 401
Kernersville, North Carolina 27285

Book design by
D.L.Shaffer
Cover Concept and design by
Joanne Clarey and David Shaffer

First Edition

ISBN:09768108-7-5

This book is dedicated to all the good people in the small villages
around the world. And to my mother
Margaret Johnson Herbold who would have
loved Hummingbird Falls.

ACKNOWLEDGEMENTS

My thanks to the very talented and supportive Triad Round Table
of Writers: Dixie Land, Dave Jakubsen, Helen Goodman, Lynette
Hall Hampton, John Staples, Dave Shaffer, and E.D. Joyner. My
gratitude to artist Anne Garland who continued to smile through
countless revisions of the cover until we found the right one.

Greenberg Daily Sun, July 1, 2006

FIREWORKS IN HUMMINGBIRD FALLS
ON JULY 3

Did you hear about the two cannibals who were eating a clown? One says to the other: "Does this taste funny to you?"

And so we begin summer. The kids are out of school, the vacationers and visitors are here in droves, the heat and humidity are back and the grass continues to grow. Enjoy, enjoy, enjoy!

On July 3 the Hummingbird Falls Area Chamber of Commerce intends to light up the skies with Hummingbird Falls' own fireworks display going off at 9 p.m. Ice cream, popcorn, glow necklaces, balloons and other fun stuff will be available.

Have a safe and happy Fourth and remember what Independence Day is all about between the fireworks, the cookouts, the partying, the vacations, and whatever. It's why we can enjoy all of these things.

1

The village of Hummingbird Falls was easing its way from spring to early summer. The rivers and streams had crested from snow melt and bellowed downhill with rowdy rapid roars. By late June most were safely encased within their boulder strewn banks. If the weather stayed clear and the hurricanes stayed off shore, the rivers would continue to slowly subside, unlike last year when rain swollen rivers threatened to flood the entire valley.

Even the Crooked River in The White Mountain State Park on Hummingbird Falls' northern border was shallow enough to expose the bit of muddy shore and quiet eddy where a body would come to rest, bobbing in the freezing cold water.

Brooks burbled through the woods surrounded by unfurling ferns, fiddleheads and snowy white May flowers. New lime green leaves fluttered in front of the dark spruces and pines of the dense forest below the timber line. The great mountains' tips, still snow covered, shimmered in the sun like white spires reaching up into a sapphire heaven.

Hummingbirds returned to the mountain glens with the robins, warblers, vireos, bluebirds and other migratory species. The Ruby Throated Hummingbirds nested once again in the greenery along the great cascades, named after them. Their tiny bodies whirled like sparkling gem stones through the mist created by white water hurtling over the huge rocks and dropping with a crash down to the next set of falls.

Fox danced in the hay fields, nosing for mice and voles. The black bears and their cubs emerged from their caves high up in the mountains and hungry, dug roots, ate buds and scavenged whatever they could find. Does with their long legged spotted fawns nibbled newly sprouted hay at the edges of meadows. Beavers worked to repair winter wrecked dams and feasted on green water shoots and brand new buds. Eagles soared, mosquitoes whined, bees hummed, chipmunks scurried, raccoons rambled, skunks slunk and owls flew with the bats at night. The black flies were thick. Hummingbird Falls was just about to burst into summer.

The human population of Hummingbird Falls emerged too, from cabin fever, the long dark frigid days of winter, snow mounds and spring muck and prepared for summer. Wood for next winter was already cut and twitched out of wood lots and lay drying in the spring sun. The villagers had beaten and rolled the woolen rugs, replaced insulated drapes with perky cotton curtains and packed heavy quilts, long underwear, wool pants and sweaters in cedar closets to wait for another season. They removed storm windows and put up screens, placed rockers on porches and tilled their gardens, planting seeds of early peas, spinach, radish and lettuce.

The little white cottage on Mountain Road, spring cleaned too, waited empty, for the strange new family from New York to move in with all their belongings, dysfunctions and secrets.

Hummingbird Falls' villagers kicked up their heels like colts in the pastures. Freed to the outdoors after a long winter, they gossiped at the Pastry Shop, renewed friendships and planned activities, made mischief, worshipped at the Little Church on Sundays, drank and danced at the Falls Bar and Grill and enjoyed their little village shops, parks and greenways during the brief time between seasons when tourists left them in peace.

Soon enough visitors from outside would arrive in Hummingbird Falls and change the peaceful mountain village in ways no one could anticipate and few would ever forget.

The folks who lived in Hummingbird Falls year round did so because their families settled here generations ago as farmers, trappers or foresters or because they loved the mountain beauty that surrounded their hamlet. With spring, residents reveled in the awakening of their natural surroundings. They walked the hills and trails and marveled at the changes nature had wrought. They spotted the spore and scat that revealed that they were not the only inhabitants of this enchanting environment.

They reverently studied the bones that emerged this year as they did every year when the snow drifts melt down. Not every creature lived through the hunting season of the late fall and the tough winter in the mountains. The new green weeds and budding bushes created a contrasting backdrop for the creamy white of skulls and leg bones, bleached beige of antlers and curved line of vertebrae. Soon the bones would lay buried under the deep mantle of myrtle, lush wild flowers and thick wild honeysuckle vines. The villagers lived with the constant reminder of the close relationship between seasons and the heart breaking inevitability that the darkness of death shadowed even the lush spring birth of life.

2

Jean white and Alma Groton sneaked out of the deli door and looked up and down the village street.

"They've disappeared," whispered Jean.

"They must have jumped into a car and sped off fast," Alma whispered back. "What should we do, call the police?"

"I don't know. Do you think what I think?"

"Absolutely. That man's going to kill some woman, right?"

"Right, just because the woman he was with told him to get rid of her."

"Right, Jean. So what are we going to do?"

"Well, first let's get off this street as fast as we can. We can talk while we walk over to my house. And keep your voice down. I don't want anyone to overhear us talking."

"Right," said Alma, scurrying along beside Jean.

"Well, the right thing to do, I suppose, is to tell the police. But what if they don't catch him and he learns that we're the witnesses? We could be endangering our families if he came hunting for us. You know, like on television, the bad guy always has to kill the witnesses to protect himself."

"Oh gosh, I didn't think of that," said Alma. "We can't go to the police then. But how can the police stop the murder if they don't know about it?"

"We could call them anonymously."

"But maybe they'll think it's just a crank call, if we don't leave our names. And we can't tell them we overheard the man and woman talking at the deli because Reggie will tell them we were just in there."

"Hmmm. Let me think," said Jean as they turned up the stone walk to Jean's house. The two women entered the house and headed for the kitchen. Jean filled the teapot and silently waited for the water to boil. Then, still thinking, she poured the hot water into her blue willow teapot. She added several spoonfuls of loose green tea and sat down at the table with Alma.

"I've got it. Let's tell Ellie Hastings, the librarian. She's the one who helped the police solve the murders of Alice and Josie last summer. She's brave enough and after all she doesn't have a family here to worry about."

"Jean, that's a great idea. Ellie loves mysteries, solving riddles and following clues. She told me so herself last week when I was in the library getting books. She's recommended some wonderful mystery books to me."

"Then that's our plan. Tomorrow morning. First thing. We'll meet at the library and turn this whole mess over to Ellie."

"Right. I feel better already," said Alma pouring a cup of tea for Jean and herself. "We'll let her figure out what the best thing to do is. After all, everyone knows she's just like that Miss Marple in Agatha Christie's mystery books, the perfect village sleuth. Let's just pray, we're not too late."

3

The mud season was almost over, but Ellie Hastings still pulled on her dark green Wellingtons whenever she left her new cabin on Foster's Brook. Her lawn, seeded last fall, was just starting to fill in around the perennial beds she had prepared, but mud was still lurking everywhere, sucking on her boots as she left her footprints behind her.

At least three mornings every week she and her beloved mutt Buddy departed from their home, drove their long dirt driveway to the Falls Road, passed by the magnificent Hummingbird Falls and then continued downhill toward the village. She had accepted the temporary assignment of Village Librarian until a more proper replacement could be found for ex-librarian Pauline Hayes who was now residing at the State Prison for Women.

Retired early from teaching High School English in a city suburb, Ellie planned to garden, paint, read mysteries and write poetry in her leisure time. Her middle aged years hadn't slowed her down in any way. Straight backed, five feet seven inches, with a comfortable layer of fat, most people described Ellie as healthy looking, although others might call her chubby or pleasingly plump. Her hair was still a soft brown, just sprinkled with a few silver strands and her face was smooth and wrinkle free except around her blue eyes, which were framed with wire rimmed glasses.

So far this spring she'd been too busy decorating her new cabin, landscaping and getting settled in to pursue her creative arts. Now that the Village Council asked her to take over the library, she wasn't sure when she'd get back to them.

Truth be told, Ellie was grateful for the library assignment. She thrived on meeting and helping people and loved hearing the chitchat and news that came to her tiny, tidy desk situated by the front door of the old shingled library that sat in the center of the village, just over the stone bridge. It was this gossip and Ellie's reputation as an inventive and trustworthy problem solver that most often got her into trouble.

This late June morning, Ellie stopped at the Pastry Shop to purchase her usual white sugared coffee and a couple of blueberry turnovers to go. As she climbed out of her old teal Subaru she saw a Uhaul truck followed by a sporty red Mustang speed up the Falls Road. She wondered if that could be the new people that Hilda Sterns, the Mountain Homes realtor, told her were moving into the little white cottage that Ellie had rented for the last ten summers. She hoped the new folks loved her cottage as much as she had and appreciated all the beautiful gardens she had labored over for the last ten summers. She had stopped by the empty cottage after the snow melted to make sure the Hummingbird feeders were full and the gardens readied for spring and summer blooming. She was hopeful the cottage would be filled with laughter and light again.

Only a few people were gathered in the Pastry Shop at this odd time between breakfast and break time. While Elizabeth, the shop owner, packed up her order Ellie stopped by her friend Mike's table to say hello.

"What's going on up at your place these days?" Ellie asked Mike, admiring his smiling tanned cragged face and the way silver was just inching its way onto his temples. A farmer all his life, Mike was in superb physical shape, muscular but slim and a very attractive six feet tall.

"Same ol', same ol'. Mucking out barns, checking fence, fixing machinery, tilling the garden, sowing the field corn, watching the weather. Got most of the cows out in the pastures now. Love to see them frisk around after a long winter indoors."

"Nice. Got your syrup done up?"

"Yep. Finished up pasting on the new labels a couple of weeks ago. Of course, I boiled down most of the sap by the beginning of April. Got a good lot this year. The sap ran perfect in March and April. Cold nights and warmer days brought it down fast. Still plenty of snow in the woods then, so I ran the horses and sleds sapping. I'm thinking of working them this summer to see if they can get in shape for the horse pull at the Freyberg Fair come fall."

"I heard you won some ribbons pulling."

"Yep, but that was years ago. I put the old work team out to pasture and got me a couple of new ones this year. Thought I'd take up horse pulling again. Course it takes a lot of work to train them to a good team."

"I'd love to see you working them out."

"Come on over any time, Ellie. You know you're more than welcome. And the apple flowers have just about set in the orchard. That's a pretty sight to see."

"Thanks Mike. I'll make sure to stop by. I planted a few apple trees of my own last fall, Cortland's, Macs and Delicious, but I don't see any flowers yet. There are some buds, so I think they made it through the winter, but I won't be having any apples for quite a few years yet."

"Your order's ready, Ellie," Elizabeth called out. "I think you have some early customers over at the library. They've been there a while."

"Got to go open the library, Mike. See you later."

"I put a day old cookie in there for Buddy," Elizabeth said as she waved Ellie goodbye.

As Ellie parked her car in the library lot she noticed that two women, Jean White and Alma Groton, were waiting on the library's front porch. It was unusual that in this village of 800 year round residents, or even in full tourist season when the population surged up over 2000, that someone would be waiting for the library to open. So, Ellie gathered her things and walked briskly to greet them.

"Good morning Jean. How are you Alma? What brings you out so early this beautiful morning?"

Buddy wagged his tail and grinned at the women as Ellie unlocked the door and snapped on the lights. "Come in, come in. Just let me adjust the thermostat so the room will warm up a bit. Fuel conservation, you know. I always turn the heat down when I leave, to about 55-60. Better leave your coats on for a while. It's chilly in here."

The two women stood quietly inside the door as Buddy made the rounds of the library's three rooms and then quietly lay down beside Ellie's desk on his fleece bed.

"Well, how are you?" Ellie asked. She placed her snack bag and coffee on her desk next to the latest Agatha Christie mystery she was reading, *The Body in the Library*. She just started it yesterday and didn't get any further than the first few pages to the scene where a beautiful woman was found dead in the library. Yesterday, she questioned her choice of stories since she was reading all alone in the quiet old building. It was rather spooky being a woman alone in the library reading about a dead woman in a library, but the humor of the first few pages of the mystery shook out her shivers. She was sorry she had to stop reading when the time came to close the library and head for home. She always left the mystery she was reading on her desk. When she took her breaks during the day, she picked it up and read a few more chapters. She liked having the mystery book she was reading waiting for her when she came to work, like an old friend ready to welcome her.

Ellie didn't know either of the two women standing before her very well. She had met Jean at church. Jean lived in the village and had a full time job taking care of her seven children and hard working forester husband Van. Ellie made Alma's acquaintance when she came to the library just a few weeks ago. Alma was an avid mystery reader and they enjoyed some good discussion over favorite authors and books. But other than that, Ellie knew nothing of Alma's personal life.

"We're not here to get a book," said Alma.

"That's okay. Do you want to do some research? Something I can help you with?"

"No," Jean answered. "We want to talk to you."

"Talk to me? Great. What's up?"

"We need your help on something that has nothing to do with the library."

"Well, you have my curiosity going now. What is it?"

"Alma and I discovered something. I mean, we have learned that, actually…"

Alma interrupted. "What Jean means is that we overheard someone talking. We didn't mean to. We aren't eavesdroppers. We were just in the deli aisle and these people were talking one row over. We couldn't help but hear what they said."

"What did they say?" Ellie prompted.

"Do you promise not to tell anyone?" asked Jean.

"I can't promise when I don't know what it is, Jean. If I have to tell someone, maybe I could say I heard it from a private source if that would help."

"That helps," Alma said. "We don't want to get mixed up in anything."

"Like what?"

"Like murder!" whispered Alma.

"Murder? Whose murder? What did you hear?"

Jean and Alma both started at once. "We don't know…"

Ellie stopped them. "One at a time. You first, Jean.

4

Jean sank down into an oak chair at the library table. "You don't know me too well, Ellie, but folks here in the village are aware that I'm not the gossipy type. Frankly, I'm too busy with the kids to sit around and listen to adults' chattering mouths. So what I'm going to tell you, you can be assured I heard myself, not from the grape vine."

Jean looked older than her middle forties. Her silver hair was pulled back into a tight pony tail leaving her lean sun wrinkled face, the bluish bags under her eyes and the deep furrows around her thin lipped mouth obvious to all. Being a stay at home mom to seven kids was taking its toll.

"Alma and I met up accidentally by the jelly and jam section of the deli. We had just exchanged a nice hello when we heard a loud voice coming from the cold drink area. That's one aisle over at the back of the deli."

Ellie nodded. She hoped the story was not going to be bogged down in irrelevant details. She was eager to get to the heart of this tale.

"Go on," Ellie said.

"It was a man's voice. I didn't recognize it. You didn't recognize it either, did you Alma?"

"No, never heard that voice before, to my knowledge." Alma said, quickly crossing her heart.

"The man said pretty loudly, 'What do you want?'," continued Jean.

"Then the woman said, 'To get rid of her.'," Alma added. "I'm sure she said 'get rid of her.'" Alma's plump face shook and she shivered in her bright red fleece jacket. Her black eyes were as wide open as they could get and so was her pink lipped mouth.

Jean continued. "The man said something I couldn't hear. Then he said, 'I'll take care of it.' The next thing I heard was the door slamming. We waited for a minute and then peeked around to the next aisle. No one was there. They both must have left."

"So," Ellie said. "You were in the deli and you both over heard a man and a woman talking about getting rid of some female. Is that right?"

"Yes," both women answered.

"Did you ask Reggie if he saw them and knew them?"

"No. We were too scared. We just ran out of the store and went to my house," said Jean. "We didn't even say goodbye to Reggie."

"And when was this?" Ellie asked.

"Yesterday afternoon, around 4:30," Alma answered and then chattered on nervously. "I just ran down there to pick up some jam for breakfast. Normally I do my shopping down in Greenberg at the discount warehouse super mart but I'd forgotten to pick up raspberry jam. That's Harry's and Jarrod's favorite. Billy, Cindy and Susan like the grape preserves. Oh, Harry's my husband. The rest are our kids, two boys and two girls. Not as many as seven like Jean has, but a handful, you can believe it. Four kids under seven years old. If I had to do it again…" Alma sighed and left the sentence unfinished.

Ellie sighed too. This story was taking a lot of time to tell, with all the many side stories that did not enhance the main theme.

"So," Jean continued, "we talked about it and decided to come here this morning and tell you. We heard that you're good at helping people figure out what to do in odd situations."

Ellie laughed. "Well, I don't know where you heard that, but I do tend to be rather analytical at times. That propensity helps when it comes to solving mysteries of any kind."

"Can you analyze what we heard and figure out what to do? We can't let a murder happen. Can you save the woman?" asked Alma.

"First, why didn't you call Dave?"

The two women looked at each other. They nodded and then Alma said, "Well, we wanted to call the police and tell Dave or Colby what we heard. But then we were afraid if people heard that we were the ones who had information about the killers who were running around Hummingbird Falls, we or our families might be endangered. Maybe the murderers would come after us. So, we thought telling you in confidence was a better idea. You can tell Dave about it if you want and we would be safe as anonymous informants, just like in that mystery I read last week. What was it called?"

Ellie laughed. "Oh, I see. It's okay for me to be identified, but not you."

"Oh, we didn't mean it that way. You're so brave and smart and after all you've worked with the police before. You don't have family here like we do and you know how to handle things like murder. Just look at what you did last summer. You solved that thirteen year old murder case and found Alice and Josie's killer at the same time."

"Okay, okay. Looks like you've elected me the fall guy."

"We don't want you to fall, heavens knows, Ellie. Or what ever that means. We just didn't know what else to do," said Alma.

"Well, to start with, let's not go overboard and call this a murder. Maybe you have been reading too many mysteries Alma. After all, you only overheard a piece of the conversation. What you listened to may be way out of context."

"But the woman wanted to get rid of her and he said he'd do it."

"That could mean anything, not just killing someone," Ellie said.

"I suppose so," said Jean rather disappointed.

"Like throw her out of the house?" Alma asked.

"Exactly," Ellie answered. "Or sell a boat. Boats are referred to as she's."

"I didn't think of that," said Jean.

"Me either," said Alma.

"Or maybe she wanted him to take the dog, who's a female, to the humane society for adoption."

"I definitely didn't think of that," Alma said.

"I didn't either," said Jean with a sigh.

"But I'll tell you what I'll do," Ellie said. "I'll go talk to Reggie and ask him if he saw those two people yesterday and find out what he knows about them. Reggie might be able to clear up this whole thing."

The two women smiled at each other and stood up. "Thank you, Ellie. You knew exactly how to handle this situation. That's why we came to you. Maybe we did just overreact. But I feel better that the matter's in your hands now," said Jean.

Alma added, "I hope we didn't waste your time. I mean I hope there isn't anything to analyze after all and we did waste your time. Oh, you know what I mean."

Ellie struggled for something kind to ease the women's embarrassment. "Maybe Reggie will confirm your suspicions and I'll have to investigate more. You never know how these things will turn out."

The two women seemed to brighten a bit. "Let us know what you find out, Ellie. Thank you."

Buddy saw them to the door and then lay down again.

"Get rid of her, hmmm. What did she mean by that?" Ellie mused out loud to Buddy as she took a big bite of her blueberry turnover. "And he agreed. Probably nothing, but it's an interesting choice of words. I wonder who those two were. Not that I think there's anything to it. Certainly not murder. Those women just let their imaginations go wild. Don't you think, Buddy?"

Buddy wagged his tail in response, thumping it loudly on the old wooden floor waiting for his taste of the turnover.

"But maybe at break time we'll have to get the poor dog a bone down at the deli," Ellie said to Buddy. "And ask a few questions."

5

At break time Ellie and Buddy strolled over to the Deli. They walked in the door and since Reggie was busy with a customer, they ambled around and then stopped to study the special arrangement attractively shelved and labeled: NATURALLY GROWN AND PRODUCED BY HUMMINGBIRD FALLS' RESIDENTS. Mabel Johnson's canned beets, pickles, corn and green and yellow wax beans sat next to Mike's Maple syrup, Ralph Hardin's homemade fudge, Don Sealy's pickled eggs, onions, and cucumbers and Ellen Pepper's assorted homemade preserves and cheeses. Gail Weatherby's hand knitted mittens and scarves, some carved wooden toys, birdhouses, handmade seed balls for birds and other home cooked foods and articles adorned more shelves. Larry Jacob's rod iron hangers were displayed as well. Ellie was just trying to decide between Henry's 100% natural homemade dog biscuits and the beef jerky for dogs when Reggie walked up to her.

"Morning Ellie. Good to see you. Can I help you with anything?"

"Morning Reggie. I'm going to try these dog biscuits for Buddy and I want to know if you have any dog bones out back."

"Sure do. Come over to the counter and I'll pick out a big juicy one for Buddy."

While Reggie was wrapping the bone in white butcher paper, Ellie decided to come right out with her main reason for being there today.

"Reggie, I'm just wondering. Around 4:30 yesterday, did you see a couple, a man and woman, in here?"

"Yesterday? Let me think back. 4:30. Oh, I remember. It was just about 4:30 when Jean and Alma were in here, acting pretty strangely. They left without buying anything or even saying goodbye."

"Anyone else here around that time?"

"Come to think of it, there was a man and woman who came in and went right to the back where the cold drinks are. They didn't buy anything either. Just walked back out."

"Do you know them?"

"No. Don't think so. Usually people I know stop and say hello or ask for something or at least say 'so long' on their way out. These two didn't say anything to me."

"Do you remember what they looked like?"

"Hmmm. The man was tall and stocky, black hair I think. The woman was petite, longish brown wavy hair, thin. Dressed like tourists. You know, matching workout suit, designer jeans, fancy shoes. Can I ask why you're so interested in them, Ellie?"

"I'm not really interested in them, Reggie. I just heard some folks were in here yesterday and my curiosity got the best of me."

"You mean Jean and Alma told you something about those two and you're investigating it, don't you? I thought there was something weird about the way those two women were acting. Did they overhear something?"

"Now Reggie. Don't go making a big fuss over this. I just wanted to know who this couple is. But since you don't know, I'm just going to forget it. No big deal."

"Come on, Ellie. You can tell me. Did Dave put you up to it? Are you undercover again?"

"No, no and no. I work at the library, not for the Chief of Police. I am just a retired teacher, a temp librarian and that's it."

"Well, if you say so, I'll take your word for it, but something seems a little fishy to me, you asking questions about strangers in here. When you start asking questions we all know something's up. Anyway, I'll keep my eyes open and if I see them again I'll take notes and let you know."

Ellie laughed. "Thanks Watson. You can be my right hand man in any investigation I undertake. Thanks for Buddy's bone, too. See you later."

As Ellie and Buddy walked back to the library, Ellie reached down and patted Buddy's head.

"I hope we haven't opened up a can of worms, boy. Just what we need, everyone in town thinking I'm sneaking around undercover on the look out for a couple who murdered some woman. They already think I'm like a skulker looking for night crawlers. I hope Dave doesn't get wind of it. I promised him I'd keep out of the private investigating business and leave Hummingbird Falls' mysteries up to him after all that happened last summer. If he hears that I'm nosing around trying to determine if a murder is being planned, and I didn't tell him first, he might just put me in those old stocks standing on the green."

6

The five Buckley's weren't happy. Nothing had gone right since long before they left Albany, New York, stopped in New Jersey and started the long drive to the mountains through the unusually muggy June humidity. Hours ago the bickering and blaming had stopped in the Mustang and now twelve year old Missy and her mother Millie were stone quiet, listening to

Goldie-oldie rock and roll music while they trailed the Uhaul rental truck in front of them.

The front seat of the Uhaul was uncomfortably sticky and sizzling. The air conditioner hadn't worked for the last eighty miles and Todd and the two boys, Matt, 16, and Michael, 8, were hot and sweating. They weren't talking either, lost in their own misery as they listened to country western tunes on the only station they could wheedle to play on the static packed radio.

Actually, things had been going downhill for the Buckley's for a long time. Ted Giabaldi, aka Todd Buckley, had been caught stealing from his clients' investment funds and had been fired two months ago. In order to avoid incarceration, he repaid all that he had stolen and all the rest of the Giabaldi family's savings and retirement funds now belonged to a slick lawyer and a bribable assistant DA. Declaring bankruptcy and selling their five bedroom, five bathroom house with tennis courts and pool in an upper class area of Albany, New York was the only way out of a horrible financial, social and emotional nightmare. The three kids left their pricey private schools. Plasma TV's, cars, expensive high end furnishings, antiques, jewelry, clothes and rugs went to auction.

The DA was investigating and considering filing additional charges against Giabaldi for money laundering and the IRS was looking into his tax situation, but neither had yet brought the new evidence before the grand jury. Before further legal action could be taken, Ted, his wife Lilly and their three children packed the rented truck and a used Mustang, bought with cash right off a side street car lot, with their remaining personal items. Ted and the two boys drove away in the truck with Lilly and Missy following in the Mustang. First, they headed south.

In New Jersey Ted connected with a man who owned a small printing shop, referred by his New York lawyer. The printer sold a variety of paper work, from birth certificates and social security cards to passports, driver's licenses and notarized last will and testaments. Suddenly Ted Giabaldi became Todd Buckley. Lilly became Millie Buckley. Matt, Missy and Michael kept their first names and reluctantly acquired the sire name of Buckley.

They contacted a realtor in the White Mountains and urged her to find a rental house for them as soon as possible. Millie used her lap top computer to search through listings and finally decided on a cottage in the remote village of Hummingbird Falls. They hoped the frequency of seasonal renters who visited for hiking in summer and skiing in winter would explain the Buckley's sudden appearance in the town and that the remote setting would protect them from inquisitive neighbors and legal processors.

The Buckleys drove through the night and most of the next day, arriving in Hummingbird Falls early in the morning of the last week in June. They drove under the covered bridge at the entrance to the tiny village, passed the Little Church next to the small shingled library, drove over the stone bridge and passed by the green in the center of town. They went by the post office, the art gallery and the Pastry Shop and Deli, several large inns and a golf course and continued on up the steep winding road that bordered the spectacular and famous Hummingbird Falls water cascades. After several wrong turns onto dirt roads that seemed to go no where, they found Mountain Lane and the small white cottage tucked just in front of a thick forest, miles from the nearest neighbor.

"I don't believe it," whined Millie Buckley. "Our garage was bigger than this."

She emerged from the Mustang convertible and stumbled as her three and one half inch heels met with the gravel driveway.

"Shit, if I break a heel on these shoes, that realtor will have to pay to replace them."

"What a dump," shrieked Missy, dressed in a short mini skirt and a splashy sequined top that barely covered her chest. "I'm not living here. I want to go home."

Todd climbed out of the rental truck and yelled, "Shut up both of you. Wake up Matt. Get a move on Michael. Get out of the truck now and start doing something."

Eight year old Michael was dressed in shorts and a t-shirt emblazoned with a rap singer's graffiti signature. He dropped down from the front seat of the UHaul and shook his long black hair back out of his eyes.

"Where's the pool?" he asked. "I'm hot."

His older brother, Matt, blond hair shaved in a design that spelled out the letters DXX, bare chested and dressed in baggy pants that hung down below his waist revealing his low slung boxers, slid out of the front seat and glared about. He hunched his shoulders and kicked at the gravel driveway.

"You've got to be kidding. You can't mean this. You can't drag us up here and expect us to live in some shack in the backwoods. I'm not staying. I'm on the next train out." His diamond ear studs reflected light as he swung around and stared hostilely at his parents.

"Then you'll have to walk about fifty-five miles to find the first bus station that will take you to the train," sneered his father. "In the meantime, get the back of this truck open and start unloading things. You, too, Missy."

Todd stared at the cottage. He looked at Millie. "Is this really it? Are you sure this is the place we rented? It looks really small."

"Yes, but on the computer it looked bigger. The realtor said it was all updated and big enough for a family of five."

Todd shook his head and laughed.

"Well, she took us. We paid her a year in advance, plus two months security which we can't get back until the year is up.

Let's face it. She stiffed us. Everyone's either a player or a fool. This time we sure were the fools. Most of our available cash is sucked up in this dump."

"Well, we could at least look inside. Maybe it's bigger than it looks. Fortunately there's a lot of land and no neighbors to bug us. And no one here knows us. With our name changed the IRS and the district attorney won't be able to find us. Look. There's a nice porch, plus a side screen porch, too. That's good."

Millie was trying to make the best of things, as was her nature in times of crisis. As she tottered toward the front steps of the house her heels sunk down into the soft ground with each step and before she could take another she had to pull the muddied heel out of the hole it made. By the time she reached the steps, the yard looked like it had been invaded by moles.

Missy's silver flip flops fared much better and she beat her mother to the porch steps and slammed through the unlocked front door, ignoring her father's demand that she start unpacking the UHaul.

A minute later, Todd and the boys heard a scream from inside the cottage. The front door banged open and Missy ran out.

7

"I'm not staying here. It's impossible. There's only one bathroom. Only one. No one can live with only one bathroom. There are five of us. What were you thinking of?"

Millie followed her wailing daughter out to the porch. "We'll just have to take turns. When your father and I got married, we only had one…"

"Mom. Stop with the history. Nobody cares about back in the dark ages. This is now. And I won't share a bedroom with those boys. That's illegal, isn't it? You can't make me sleep upstairs in that attic with them."

Missy sat down on the porch steps and started to work her way up to hysteria.

Her mother said, "We'll set up partitions. You'll have your privacy."

"No, Mom," Missy screamed. "I'll run away. I will."

Millie lowered herself down onto the steps. She put her head on her hands and studied her muddied feet for a few moments. Then she stood up and said,

"Listen to me, all of you. You, too, Todd. We're in a mess. This is all we have. None of us has much of a choice. Think of it as if we're in a witness protection program, only if we're found, your Dad will go to prison for a long time and the rest of us will be homeless and on the streets. So, it's either live here for a year and see what we can come up with or beg on the street. Make your choice."

No one said anything.

Millie continued, "So, then, make the best of it. And I don't want to hear any more complaining. If you have to run away, then do it. There's nothing more I can do."

Millie stamped down the steps and walked, as briskly as her high heels allowed, by her daughter, stunned sons and husband. She opened the back of the Uhaul and picked up the first box she found, turned and stumbled with it through the yard, up the steps and into the house without another word.

Meekly, each of the other family members, including sobbing Missy, followed suit.

In a few hours the Uhaul was empty and Todd drove to Greenberg to turn it in. Matt followed in the Mustang. Millie,

Michael and Missy worked to make beds up and get the kitchen in working order.

"No dishwasher. No garbage disposal. No trash compactor. No central vac. No air conditioner. No cable. No satellite dish. Only one tiny bathroom. No pool. Only one phone jack. Our bed fills the whole bedroom downstairs, so there's no room for a bureau. One tiny closet downstairs and no closets or electrical outlets up in kid's room. And no basement. There's only a dark crawl space, too damp to even store things. And, of course, no garage. This is a disaster. What are we going to do?" Millie asked Todd when he returned.

"I don't know," answered Todd. He had emptied out the trunk of the Mustang and was carrying two hunting rifles, a shotgun and boxes of ammunition.

"I guess I'll have to put these under our bed, if there isn't any storage closet that can lock."

Missy laughed. "There isn't even a closet, let alone a lock. I bet even the front door doesn't lock."

Todd took the guns into the bedroom and pushed them under the bed.

When he came back into the living room he said, "Look, no one touches those guns. Got it? No one. I don't want any accidents happening. We've got enough trouble as it is."

"Okay, Dad," the three kids answered quietly. The whole family was gathered glumly in the living room. Millie was sitting on the couch, Matt and Michael on boxes, Missy on the floor, and Todd on a kitchen chair that hadn't made it to the kitchen yet.

"While we are all together here, we might as well talk about what we're going to do," Millie said.

They all looked at her expectantly as if she might have a solution to the horrible dilemma that faced them. Their faces fell as she continued.

"These are the facts. Your father's in trouble, as you know. We can't go back or he'll go to jail. We have no money. We've changed our names so that no one will connect us with the stories that are bound to be on the news. We still have to be very careful. It's a big change for us all, but we have talked it over and decided this is the best thing to do. So, let's just get on with it and make it work."

"But Mom," whined Missy.

"Excuse me, but shut up, Missy. Whining will do no good. You're just going to have to be creative and figure out how to live with this."

"At least we don't have to go to school," said Michael. "That's a good thing."

"Sorry," answered Todd. "You have to go to the public school here. All of you. If you don't go, the authorities will be suspicious. Anyway, you have to go to school. Things will get better some day and you'll want to go to college, so you have to keep going to school."

"But what about our transcripts? They'll have our real name on them," said Matt.

"We'll just delay on the transcripts. Make something up like we lost them or give the wrong name or address of the schools and by the time the requests come back with wrong address notification, it'll be too late. You'll already be enrolled and in the middle of the quarter. Anyway, we don't have to worry about school for a couple of months."

"How'll I make any friends, up here in the woods?" Missy asked.

"When we go to the stores and the shops downtown, you'll probably run into some kids. You'll meet them, don't worry. And, I'm hoping you and Matt will get jobs for the summer, working at one of the inns or doing babysitting."

"Working? We're too young. We've never had to work before. None of my friends work. I won't do it," Missy screamed. "This is just too much."

"This isn't before, Missy. It's after. And if you want any spending money you'll just have to earn it. We don't have any extra."

"I'll never be happy again," Missy cried.

"Tell me about it," Matt mumbled.

"Do they have Little League here?" asked Michael.

"I don't know," Todd answered. "Your mom will find out. Meanwhile I have to find a job. I picked up the local paper and I'm going out to that screen porch, sit down and check out the classified ads."

Todd stood up and walked into the screen porch, pulled up a box, sat down and started to read the paper.

The others just looked at one another and slowly one by one left to unpack their belongings. Matt hesitated as he passed by his parents' room. When his mom went into the kitchen and Missy and Michael climbed the steps to the attic, he darted into the room. He kneeled down and pulled out the shotgun and fumbled around under the bed until he found the proper ammunition for the gun. Then he turned and ran out the back door and into the woods.

8

Ellie started the closing of the library at 4:00, pleased with the steady stream of readers that had made the day go by so quickly. She had met so many people while working at the library and having a town job helped her feel more like a local resident than a transplanted outsider.

She straightened the library shelves section by section. She was just at the beginning of the mystery section when she noticed an Agatha Christie mystery, *A Pocket Full of Rye*, upside down. When she pulled the book out to reshelf it, she spotted a piece of paper sticking out from between the pages. She unfolded the paper and read the big block letters typed across the page.

THIS IS FOR REAL.
FOLLOW THE CLUES OR YOU WILL BE SORRY.
THIS IS NOT A JOKE. IF YOU DO NOT SOLVE THE
RIDDLES, SOMETHING VERY BAD WILL HAPPEN.
CLUE ONE: MISS M. LOVED TO DRINK HERS,
BUT IT KILLED OTHERS. YOU WILL HAVE TO DRIVE
TO LOCATE YOURS AND TO FIND THE NEXT CLUE.
WHEN YOU GET THERE LOOK DOWN AND FIND
THE GOLD.

Ellie read the note again. She turned it over. It was blank on the other side. What did this note mean? Who could have left it? Was the note meant for her or was it hidden waiting for whoever took out the mystery book next? Maybe it didn't matter who found it or when. How long had that piece of paper been there tucked in the book? Did the warning have anything to do with what Jean and Alma overheard? Or was it just someone's idea of a joke? Had one of her friends put the note in the book for fun and to stir things up a little? Ellie had straightened the shelves just two days ago and hadn't noticed the book upside down then. So, someone must have left the note yesterday or today. What a mystery.

Ellie sat down at her desk and looked up who had last taken out *A Pocket Full of Rye*. John Staples, the Hummingbird Falls Newspaper editor, signed the book out last month and returned it on time, fourteen days later. It hadn't left the library since then. Could John be the author of the note? Did he stick that paper in the book and then return the book without her noticing it? That seemed unlikely. She checked all the returned books carefully. And John loved reading mysteries, but he wasn't the type to leave secrets messages about in strange places. Perhaps something was going on with him that Ellie didn't know about. She'd have to check him out, either by going directly to his office or by asking some subtle questions the next time she was in the Pastry Shop.

Ellie looked over the files to see who had been in the library over the last two days and had checked out books. Anyone of those people could have left the note. Or for that matter, maybe someone came in and left the note but didn't bother to take out a book. So the clue writer could be anyone who was even in the library over the last two days. Or could the writer of the note be one of the several people at the Town Hall or on the Library Committee who had keys to the building? And did one of those key holders sneak into the library and leave the note after library hours? If so, why? What a puzzle.

Ellie decided to make a list of everyone who had taken out a book and everyone else who she remembered being in the library over the last two days. The list wasn't very long. Only sixteen people had stopped by the library that she could remember and that included Jane and Alma today who weren't out of her sight for a minute. Then there were the six keys to the library that she knew of. She had one. The Town secretaries, Debbie and Bonnie, kept three of the library's keys locked in the safe in the town office. The Library Committee Chairwoman, Helen Martin, had one and so did Glen Watkins, Director of the Historical Society. So eliminating Jean and Alma, herself and the three keys in the safe, ten possible suspects remained. That reminded her of another Agatha Christie mystery, *And Then There Was None*. She shivered. Ten people die in that mystery. Suddenly she felt very frightened as she and Buddy sat alone in the quiet old library. She looked around to make sure they really were alone and then walked over, put the closed sign in the window and locked the library door.

9

Ellie studied the note closely under her desk lamp. The first part of the riddle wasn't too difficult to decipher. Miss M. had to be the well loved heroine of several Agatha Christie's mysteries, the famous Miss Marple. Ellie remembered that Miss Marple's favorite drink was tea. Ellie flipped through the first couple of pages of the book, *A Pocket Full of Rye*. In the very first chapter, *Death by Tea*, a woman dies from drinking poisoned tea. Oh dear, was the writer of the note warning her that someone in Hummingbird Falls was going to be poisoned by drinking tea? Or was she the intended victim? What would happen if she didn't solve the riddle?

The second part of the note was more difficult to decode. The note said, "You will have to drive to the one to locate yours." That sentence didn't seem to make any sense. The finder of the note would have to drive to find hers. Her what? Drive to find tea? Drive to a tea house? Drive to a house where someone drinks tea? Ellie knew a lot of tea drinkers. Sarah, the Hummingbird Falls' Postmaster, came to mind, but so did Bonnie, the secretary down at the Hummingbird Falls Town Hall, Chuck the minister at the Little Church, and several others, including herself. There was no tea house in Hummingbird Falls. Why would anyone want to drive to get tea that might be poisoned? Did the note mean she had to drive home to get her tea and that her tea was poisoned?

Ellie felt stymied. She tried to tell herself that she was taking this note far too seriously. The note was probably just an attempt to pull a joke on her by some kids, or perhaps one of her friends was teasing her, knowing how Ellie loved solving mysteries and figuring out clues.

But the warning the note's writer threatened her with just seemed too serious to ignore. Maybe it wasn't a joke. And if it wasn't, she better get busy and figure the darn riddle out. Even if it was just a joke, figuring out the riddle wouldn't hurt. She would show whoever wrote it that she was clever enough to solve it.

Even though she was feeling edgy and a little frightened, Ellie was also intrigued. She loved solving mysteries. Her curiosity, intelligence, and high level of energy created the perfect qualities for an expert investigator. She would keep at it until she had the riddle all figured out, whether it turned out to be a joke or not. And if it turned out to be as real as the writer claimed, she would deal with that part when it happened.

"Drive to the one." What was the one? One what? Ellie tried to put the second clue with the first. Miss Marple drank hers and that was tea. But the reader of the note would have to drive to tea. Drive to get tea. Where could she drive to get to a tea place, a site of tea?

"Whoops!" Ellie called out. Buddy jumped to his feet and wagged his tail. "That's it, Buddy. I have to drive to a t. The best known t in town is the T up at Black Bear Bridge. I bet that's it. I've got it."

Ellie did a little dance and Buddy jumped up and down with her. They were so excited they knocked over the waste basket and spilled papers all over the floor. As Ellie bent down to pick up the mess, Buddy covered her face in kisses.

"Okay Buddy, the rest of the shelving can wait 'til next time. I'm just going to finish cleaning up our mess, turn down the heat, and shut the lights out and we'll be off to the T at Black Bear Bridge."

Ellie and Buddy piled into the car and headed up the Falls Road, turned down The Old Town Farm Road and drove until they came to the bridge at the end of The Old Town Farm Road where it intersected with the Outlook Notch Road in a perfect T. Everyone in the village referred to this spot as "The T."

Ellie parked the car on the side of the road and jumped out.

"You wait here Buddy. I'll be right back."

She studied the note again. "LOOK DOWN AND FIND THE GOLD." Ellie walked back to the bridge and peered over its side. She saw the Black Bear River roaring downhill, crashing over boulders and making white water waves. She saw the stones and green bushes edging the river.

"What am I supposed to be looking for?" she asked. "I don't think anyone has ever found gold in these rivers. Mica, yes, and fool's gold, but real gold? I don't think so."

She scanned the bridge itself, then leaned far over and examined the outside of the bridge. There were scrubbed out remains of some old graffiti, but otherwise nothing looked out of the ordinary. Ellie eyed the sides of the river, the road bed of the bridge. Nothing. The note must have been just a joke some kid put in the book after all. Oh well, it was a good gag; it had fooled her into driving out here. But she had to admit that she was a little disappointed too. Following a string of riddles or clues would have been a great adventure. As long, of course, that it didn't involve real danger or dead bodies.

She turned back toward the car and walked slowly toward it. When she reached the edge of the bridge just where it met the road in a T she saw something that sparkled on the asphalt. She kneeled down to look closer. A tiny gold arrow was painted on the road and pointed toward the right side. Ellie followed the direction of the arrow with her eyes. And there it was, sitting in the shadow of huge piece of granite rock, just waiting to be found. The note writer was serious after all.

10

Next to a large granite rock sat a china cup, resting on a matching saucer. Blue Willow patterned, it was chipped and well used. Ellie picked it up carefully, using a tissue from her pocket, mindful that she didn't want to destroy any forensic evidence or smear any possible finger prints. Dave Shaffer, Hummingbird Falls Police Chief, drummed that knowledge into her head last summer when they were working on a double mystery and a double murder case.

Inside the cup was a folded note. The size and color of the paper looked similar to the first note she found. Ellie took the paper out and then wrapped up the cup and saucer the best she could with the tissues from her pocket. Then she carefully set the cup and saucer down on the ground and unfolded the note. It read:

I TOLD YOU THIS WAS FOR REAL.
YOU GOT HERE SO YOU'RE VERY SMART.
NOW YOU MUST FIND THE CROOKED HEART.
HURRY OR VALUABLE TIME WILL BE LOST.
AND YOU'LL BE SORRY AT WHAT IT COSTS.

Ellie turned the note over. Blank on the back, just like the first note. She read it again. The message didn't mean anything to her, but it scared her. This was no teenage joke. And no friend of hers would want to frighten her to death by threatening her with an outcome of being sorry about the cost of not solving a riddle in a certain amount of time. Suddenly she felt a shiver run down her back, the kind of shiver that usually warned her that someone was right behind her, watching. Ellie whirled around. Nobody was there. She slowly studied the bushes, the woods and the edges of the road as she backed towards her parked car. She saw nothing out of the ordinary. But the woods suddenly seemed sinister and darker than normal for this time of the afternoon.

"Guess I'm spooked," she said out loud. And then she yelled, "Anyone there? Hello. Come on out. This really isn't funny."

Nothing stirred. The only sound was the roar of the river and the wind ruffling through the trees.

Ellie picked up the cup and saucer and walked quickly back to the car. She got in and locked the door. She carefully placed the cup and saucer and the note in the glove compartment. Buddy was sleeping. She woke him up by patting his head rather vigorously.

"I should have taken you with me, boy. But since you stayed sound asleep, I guess I'm just imagining that someone was there, watching me. Otherwise, you'd be barking wouldn't you?"

Buddy looked at her quizzically. He licked her face and gave a little bark.

"Too little, too late old boy." Ellie glanced around one more time and then started the car and headed for home.

"The crooked heart. Buddy, we have to find a crooked heart. I haven't a clue. Do you? But first, we're going to have a snack. We'll figure out this second riddle while we're nibbling on something."

Ellie and Buddy made their way back across the mountain and down to their comfy cabin. Remembering Miss Marple and *Death by Tea*, Ellie carefully inspected the unopened raspberry tea package she took from her cupboard. Only after she determined the box was totally untampered with did she make her tea. Several cookies completed her snack. Buddy munched on his day old cookie from the pastry shop. They talked about what the crooked heart could mean while they ate, but didn't get anywhere but more confused.

So since there was still plenty of time for Ellie to work in her gardens before darkness fell, she cleared the table and quickly changed into her gardening garb which consisted of her old jeans, Wellingtons, a flannel shirt and a bug net over her head to fend off the fierce black flies. She had been waiting all day to be outside in her yard, so she put away all thoughts of the crooked heart, couples in the deli who were planning to murder a woman, one already dead woman found in Agatha Cristie's fictional library and another poisoned by tea and the two mysterious riddles. Ellie and Buddy trekked outside to the gardens in the backyard.

The area had been cleared of trees, a path cut down to the brook, and beds for perennials, annuals and vegetables dug around the perimeter. Ellie already started her planting back in May and little radishes, carrots, peas, lettuce, spinach, onions and nasturtiums, had popped their stems up out of the rich soil and were opening their true leaves to the sun between the fading daffodils, crocuses and tulips. Ellie always planted her vegetables and flowers together, a kind of companion gardening. She liked the look of kale mixing with the later blooming phlox, tomatoes climbing next to delphinium, cucumbers blooming around marigolds, beans, yellow, red and green, wrapping around trellises of red and pink roses. The diverse mixture captured her fancy and confounded many of the pests that would ordinary feast on her plants if they were gathered in like beds.

Today Ellie was going to plant some seeds that needed warmer soil to flourish. She opened up the bush bean packet and using her finger made an indentation about an inch deep in the soil and then drew a line in the enriched soil that followed the curve of the bed. Then she placed the beans in the dirt one by one about an inch apart, covered them carefully and pressed down the soil over them. She set her hand made stakes, painted with pictures of bush beans, at either end of the curved row. Then she gently watered the newly planted beans.

She worked planting cucumbers, zucchini, squash and pumpkins mixed with marigolds and nasturtiums in much the same way until the sun began to slip behind the trees and a chilly breeze blew in from the mountains. After she rinsed off her hands under the hose she turned and admired her yard. She felt so at peace here and loved making this new place her own.

Just as she stepped into the back screen porch with Buddy she heard the warning racket of cawing crows. She looked out toward the forest. Something was upsetting the crows but she couldn't see anything out there. The crows kept up their noisy caution; their sounds moved closer to Ellie's cabin.

Suddenly a doe crashed through the under brush and into the back yard. She looked panicked, her tail up, her head held high. She was winded, but after a few seconds continued running across the yard and disappeared into the woods on the other side. Ellie stared into the woods, trying to see what the doe was running from. She heard the sound of a pursuer breaking branches and snapping twigs. It was coming closer. Buddy whined then started a low growl deep in his throat. His hair rose up around his haunches. He stood rigid, eyeing the woods.

Then he began to bark, growl and bark.

"Good boy, Buddy, you tell 'em," Ellie encouraged.

Buddy responded with more barking, running back and forth across the length of the porch. After a few moments he stopped. Ellie and Buddy listened. The crows were silent. The woods were silent. Not even the sounds of the evening birds, crickets or peepers sang out into the dusk. The unusual quiet was unsettling and Ellie frowned. Someone or something was out there. The crows, the doe, and Buddy and she heard the crashing about. Now all was still. Where was the noise maker? Was it still out there watching? Was it an animal or a human? What was going on?

11

Ellie saw the first of the evening bats flit across the backyard, starting its nightly meal of mosquitoes, black flies and moths. Gradually, the peepers began to sing again, then the crickets. Ellie heard a late chic a dee dee dee as she stood gazing at the first star of the evening caught in the darkening blue of the sky.

"Buddy, you're the best dog anyone ever had. Look what you did. You restored peace to our little part of the world. I love you."

Ellie kneeled down and hugged Buddy and rubbed his tummy just where he liked it. He thumped his tail on the slate floor of the porch and licked Ellie's face. Ellie scanned the back yard. She saw nothing she should worry about.

"Okay boy, excitement over for today. Time for us to eat."

She locked the door and set the motion lights on. If an animal was hiding out in the woods, fine, that was the critters' domain. But if it was a human predator, the worst kind and definitely unnatural, and he stepped onto her land, the spot lights would announce his arrival and warn Ellie so she could take the proper action.

After dinner, Buddy happily chewed his bone and Ellie sat down with a pad of paper. She wrote "Crooked Heart" at the top of the paper. Then she started writing down any word that came to her mind when she thought of crooked hearts, crooked or heart. She had played this word association game many times when trying to figure something out. Her list grew long and she grew irritated. Nothing she came up with seemed to make any sense. She was no closer to figuring this riddle out than she had been when she first found it. Suddenly she noticed the time.

"Oh my goodness. It's 11:00 and way past our bedtime. I don't know where the time went," she said to Buddy. She checked to make sure the doors were locked and the windows were secure as well. Then she prepared for bed and climbed into her side. Buddy was already asleep on his side, little snores declaring his pleasure. Ellie picked up her dictionary determined to work on the riddle some more. She found the word crooked and started to read the definitions. Her eyes became heavy, too heavy to read anymore and soon she dropped the book onto the floor. She was sound asleep when the first dim sounds of shots echoed softly around the valley.

12

Sarah was raging. "I'm telling you Ellie, something crazy's going on. Last night I woke up again hearing those blasted gun shots. Some loony's running around in the woods shooting at things, and for all I know, at people, too. I swear a bullet hit my back wall. I heard a shot and then a thud. I called the police first thing this morning and told them to come over and check to see if there's a bullet hole in the back of my house."

"Did you talk with Dave?" Ellie asked, rubbing her eyes and trying to see the clock without her glasses. "Sarah, it's only 5:30. The sun isn't even up yet."

"Sorry to wake you, but I'm really upset. When I called the police, the dispatcher said they'd send someone over when they had a chance this morning, but it might not be 'til later on because Dave and Colby have a lot of things to do, getting ready for the holiday and all. So I called Larry. He's the village road maintenance chief after all. Anyway, he said he'd check it out with Dave and come right over if Dave okayed it."

"Holiday?" Ellie asked.

"The fourth of July, silly."

"But it isn't the fourth yet, is it?"

"No, but you know all the odds and ends that have to be done in the village to get ready. And Dave being Chief and Colby the only other officer, they're spread thin setting up parking areas, checking on the safety of the firework site, putting out traffic blockades around Main Street, checking out the backgrounds of the vendors and who knows what else. Too busy to tend to the likes of me," Sarah harrumphed.

Ellie didn't comment. She knew Sarah would continue at her own pace.

"Anyway, I have to go to put up the flag, bring in the mail and open the post office in an hour, so I wanted to call you before I left. Have any of you up there on the mountain heard any shots? Or seen anything unusual? I know you have a nose for strange happenings and mysteries and I think this qualifies as one."

"Who me? Nosy? Sarah, how can you say that? Look, I don't ask for these things to come calling me. I'm not on a quest for danger and excitement. I'm just a quiet retired lady English teacher who spends my time writing poetry, painting pictures, gardening, playing with my dog and working three days at the library. Anyway, nosy or not, I can hardly think at this hour. I haven't had anything to eat yet. I haven't even had my coffee."

"Now, Ellie, calm down. I didn't say you were nosy, but you can't deny that you do seem to end up in the center of most anything unusual that happens around here. Now, have you or have you not heard any gun shots?"

Ellie sighed. She could just imagine the jubilation of justification in Sarah's voice if Ellie confessed to her about the two mysterious riddles she had found. Sarah would connect them to all the crazy things she said were going on and get even more upset. So, Ellie decided to keep the riddles a secret for now, even though Sarah would be an excellent assistant for decoding the clues. No sense in feeding Sarah's already formed ideas about Ellie's personality type. But Ellie knew that Sarah rarely gave up without getting what she wanted. So she sleepily attempted to cooperate with her.

"Okay, Sarah, now that you mention it, I have woken up the last couple of nights thinking I heard something outside and

Buddy was whining. It might have been gun shots that woke Buddy and me, but once I was awake I didn't hear anything that sounded like a gun and I went back to sleep."

Ellie thought about telling Sarah about the doe who was chased from the woods, but decided that incident probably didn't have anything to do with the guns Sarah was hearing.

"Well, keep listening and let me know if you hear anything. I've got a bad feeling about this and you know my bad feelings unfortunately turn out to be right more often than not."

"I'll try to pay more attention, Sarah. Thanks for the warning."

Ellie hung up the phone wondering if the disturbances over the last several nights had involved gun fire. She did remember hearing the far away rumble of thunder, but instead of thunder bangs had the noises really been the shots Sarah was talking about? And that frightened doe that dashed across the back yard. Could it have been running from someone with a gun?

Certainly some strange things were happening. Sarah might be right to be suspicious. Maybe she should get together with Sarah tomorrow. Sarah had been helpful in the past when Ellie needed some wise advice and a companion to help investigate mysterious things. Maybe the gun shots and the murderous couple in the deli, the clue in the mystery book, the riddle in the cup and saucer, the crooked heart, the sense someone was watching her and the frightened doe running from something or someone had some connection. Yes, she would arrange a meeting with Sarah. Together they'll figure out what was going on. And if telling Sarah about the riddles meant that Ellie's reputation would grow like Pinocchio's nose, then so be it. At least Ellie wouldn't be alone with a riddler who was up to no good as far as she could tell. And with that thought Ellie snuggled up next to Buddy and fell back asleep.

13

State bureau of Investigation Agent Bill Crandall followed Park Ranger Ralph Walters down the winding dirt trail for over a mile as it declined steeply. This was rough hiking, even for an experienced and fit outdoorsman like Crandall. Deep woods lined both sides of the hiking trail clear down to the stream bed. Tough roots and sharp stones burst through the slippery earth making every step dangerous. Young hemlocks hedged the dirt path, fronting for the tall white pines and spruce that covered the land known as the Outreach, a remote part of The White Mountain State Park.

When they arrived at the bottom of the trail, Walters stopped, pointed, and then stepped aside so Crandall could take the lead.

"I didn't go any farther than this. I could see she was dead. I didn't want to mess up the ground or disturb anything."

"You did right, Ralph," Crandall said. "Let's just stay here while I do a visual."

Crandall took a digital camera out of his pocket and started snapping pictures as he rotated from left to right. After a few moments, he said, "Okay, walk just where I walk. We'll take it slow."

"I could wait here if you'd rather."

"It's better if you come with me, if you don't mind. I could use a good witness."

"Okay. Just tell me what to do."

Crandall eased down the incline, keeping his eyes on the trail. He stopped and turned around.

"When did it last rain here?"

"Late last night we had about a half inch of rain. That's why the trail's so slippery."

"What time last night?"

"I guess it was actually around 3-3:30 this morning."

"So there are no footprints or signs of moved rocks. The rain washed out any traces."

The two men climbed down until they were on the rocky shore of the Crooked River which ran from springs at the top of Outreach Mountain down thousands of feet through the forest before racing through the bottom of this gulley. The Crooked River split in two here, leaving a heart shaped island, before it continued down to join other mountain brooks, rivers and streams to form the mighty Algonquin River that eventually runs into the Atlantic Ocean, hundreds of miles away.

The body laid face up. Brown sandy muck edging a shallow eddy set away from the center of the fast rushing river anchored the corpse opposite the small island. Mud and washed up branches and brush prevented the water from pulling the corpse further downstream. Animals and insects had nibbled and bitten the exposed flesh. Birds or other predators had plucked out the eyes leaving dark staring hollows. But the body had not yet begun to decompose.

Leaning closer, Crandall saw a white female in her forties. She was rather thin and about five feet, four inches tall. Her lean high cheek boned face was partially obscured by wet brown hair that washed back and forth with the rise and fall of the streams' spring torrent of water. Other than the nibbles and the empty eye sockets, there were no obvious signs of violence. The corpse was dressed in what Crandall guessed was an expensive exercise outfit, matching top and bottom. A pair of

Nike cross trainers completed the outfit. She looked as if she was taking a nap, except that one didn't nap in a cold mountain river, her skin was a milky white blue and, of course, she was not breathing.

After he studied the corpse, Crandall widened his focus to the area adjacent. "Can you tell me what made those marks in the mud next to the body?"

Ranger Walters bent down and studied the spore. "Looks like squirrel, raccoon, maybe some mice or small voles, a fox and a couple of different birds, good sized birds like crows or turkey buzzards were here in the early hours today."

Walters straightened up. "Do you think she fell on the trail, hit her head, and then lay in that cold water until she died? She'd be dead from exposure in just a little while in that freezing water." He looked up at the SBI agent. "Do you think that's what happened, she froze to death?"

Crandall shook his head no. "That woman didn't die of exposure. I think she was shot."

The Ranger stared at Crandall. "Shot?" He looked back down at the body. "How can you tell that? There's no blood, no bullet holes. She looks perfectly fine. Except of course, she's dead."

"Simple," Crandall answered. "See her color? No blood in her. She bled out. I bet the Medical Examiner will find a bullet hole in her back."

The Ranger studied the dead woman's body. "Yeah, I see what you're saying. She certainly is pale. Do you want to turn her over to check it out?"

"We'll have to wait for the M.E. and the forensic guys to tell us that, Ralph. Let's get that tent over her for now. The lab boys won't be here for a while and I want to protect the body from any more animal contamination. Just be careful where you walk. Put these booties over your boots and don't touch anything.

We'll cover her over with the tent and then I want this trail shut down. I'll stretch crime scene tape around this area to keep everyone not connected with the investigation out."

The two men went about the work of securing the site and then hiked back the long mile to the trail entrance. The wooden box staked at the trail's start held a clip board with a pencil secured to it with a long piece of string. A sign with the White Mountain State Park logo on top stated:

"All hikers sign in here before using this trail."

The clipboard paper was blank. No one had signed in or out.

Crandall tied yellow crime scene tape around the entrance to the trail and the sign in box.

"Don't touch this box or clipboard. Maybe some prints we can pick up. I'll have to make sure that all the Rangers' prints are on the data base so they can be eliminated. Does every hiker sign in?"

"I wish I could say they do. Most do. Some day hikers just start walking and don't bother to sign in. Nobody signed in after Sunday when I was last here. I picked up the list then. Only a few names were on it. I have the list back in the office. All those who signed in, signed out after finishing the trail. It's a loop trail that goes up Mount Black and then circles around back by the marshy land and then crosses the stream at Crooked Heart Island where it, er, she is, and then joins up to the section that comes back here.

"I told you, I have no idea who this woman is, er was. All the campers and hikers are checked in and out through the Main Gate. The gate is guarded 24/7. And no one has reported a missing person. She must have come in some way other than the gate. There are a couple of trials that originate on private land and cross over the boundary into the park, but they are clearly marked and used rarely and then only by locals who know about them. Those trails aren't even marked on the map. Maybe the people she came in with killed her and then left her behind. They must have exited and signed her out along with the rest of their group."

"Or," said Crandall, "Someone brought her in, but didn't sign her in."

"Well, even if she was a guest, she'd have to register." The Ranger looked at Crandall's face. "Oh, I get what you mean. The killer could have brought her in already dead, hidden in gear, and then dumped her down the trail. Hmmm, that would take some doing. That's a mile trek over some pretty tough territory. And to carry someone? She's got to be a hundred pounds at least. I think it would take someone pretty strong and he'd have to be in very good shape. Plus, he'd probably have to do it in the dark to avoid being seen."

Crandall just nodded. "Well she got down there somehow. I guess we're going to have to find out how as well as who and why."

He started to walk to his beat up Dodge pick up. He didn't look like the seasoned investigator he was. Crandall could have been any middle aged woodsman, in his plaid woolen shirt, blue jeans and LL Bean boots. His cap read John Deere Tractors. His stocky frame moved with some hesitation, as if arthritis had already begun to set in his joints. His face was weathered, tanned and wrinkled, setting off his intense gray eyes, eyes that took in everything around him.

"I'm going to have to see the list of everyone who checked into the park in the last week," he called to Walters. "And I want to talk to the gate keepers and any of the other Rangers who were on duty."

Crandall stopped next to his truck and looked at the forest around him. It was so thick that he couldn't see if the sky was cloudy or clear, so dense that he can only see a few feet into the woods.

This huge park was a gift from a past Governor whose wealthy family had acquired the property from the Passamaquody Indians, old time trappers and bankrupt paper companies. When the Governor died, he willed all the land to the state to be used for all people. The conditions of his bequest were that the land was to remain pristine, free from any logging, unimproved. The single road that looped around the park was rough dirt and purposely provided no pull offs and few scenic views for tourists. Visitors had to hike in this park if they wanted to see the magnificent vistas.

Only tenting was permitted unless one reserved one of the few rustic lean-tos scattered along streams, lakes, and open fields. There were no facilities for showering. Outhouses, pit latrines, were provided only in the camp grounds. There were no water facilities. All drinking water had to be carried in. All trash had to be packed out by the campers. There were no trash bins. The park did not allow hunting, RVs, pets, motorcycles, motor boats or snowmobiles. People who chose this wilderness park came to hike, to see panoramic views and wildlife very few others have seen, to climb Outlook, one of the highest peaks in the East, and to visit the Appalachian Trail that began in Georgia, continued through this park and ended at the peak of Mount Kathadin at Baxter State Park in Maine. Those who came here desired freedom from the stress and technology of the modern world and the chance to be alone in a beautiful place much unchanged from centuries before. It was more likely that a hiker here would encounter a moose than another human being.

It was a perfect place for a murder.

14

Park Ranger Ralph Walters peered down at the body lying on the Medical Examiner's stainless steel autopsy table with a grim look on his face.

"She looks just like she did when I found her, except of course she had clothes on then. I didn't touch her. I didn't even go near her. Could see she was dead."

He shuffled his feet and continued chattering nervously.

"I generally take that same route every two or three days, checking on trail conditions, making sure everything's as it should be. Last time I was there was Sunday afternoon. I always walk that trail on Sunday after most of the campers have left, just to be sure everyone's accounted for. She wasn't lying there then. I crossed that river right where that body was and it wasn't there then. I would've seen a body if it were there. No one signed the trail registration since Sunday. So, when I came through that way yesterday I wasn't expecting anyone to be there."

SBI agent Bill Crandall looked away from the body and glanced at the middle aged Park Ranger. Ralph Walters was a respected Ranger, having worked in the State Park for over two decades. He'd been steadily promoted until he was now second in command. He was an entirely reliable witness. But today he was anxious and talking non-stop. Crandall guessed it was his first time watching an autopsy in the morgue.

Crandall's thoughts and Walker's words were interrupted by the Medical Examiner.

"Just as you thought," he said as he turned the body over.

Staring at them were nine holes scattered across the center of the woman's back. The holes were so close and so well defined that they resembled empty eye sockets, mimicking the horror on the victim's face.

"She was full of buck shot," said the Medical Examiner. "Looks like she got caught in a spray of it, from a single gunshot. Came from right to left, judging by the angle of penetration. Shooter wasn't too close, but not far either or the shot couldn't have penetrated as deeply as they did. Probably 50 to 60 feet at most. Double 00 shot. Instant kill. Actually, two shot pellets managed to hit her heart. She bled out."

"So you'd say the cause of death is?" Crandall asked.

"No question," the Medical Examiner replied. "She was riddled to death."

15

Dave Shaffer was groaning. Mary, his wife of 18 years, was rubbing Ben Gay onto the small of his back.

"I've finished the lower back. Do you want me to rub it up higher?"

"No, oh well, yes. Couldn't hurt I guess."

"What did you do yesterday, have to manhandle some punk?"

"No, nothing like that. It was a busy day. Mostly desk work, getting everything ready for the festivities today."

"Then what's causing the pain?" Mary persisted.

"I think it's the gun belt. It weighs a ton. I have to carry so much gear on it. It sits on my hips like a bag of concrete and when I bend or turn around it's so damned restraining."

"Can't you take some of that stuff off? Surely you don't have to have a night stick in there all the time. And you really don't need that gun, either. Nothing ever happens here that requires a gun."

Dave looked at her. "How quickly you forget. Remember last summer? I was glad I had a gun then."

Mary nodded. "I stand corrected. But that was unusual. You've only needed a gun twice in thirteen years and it's so heavy."

"Yeah, but if I don't carry one, then Colby will be the only armed officer. The load doesn't bother him. He even carries an extra bottle of pepper spray and a full bottle of water on his belt. And he never complains about it."

Mary shook her head. "Dave dear, Colby is twenty years younger than you."

"So?"

"Dave, be realistic. You aren't getting any younger and you're doing more now with all those new condos going up and retirees moving in here by the droves. Following them are the scavengers, thieves and bad guys that feed off the rich. You're going on more calls, carrying more equipment and expecting more of yourself. I think it's time for you to add someone on to the police force. There's too much for you and Colby to do by yourselves."

"What? Hire a new rookie? I've barely got Colby broken in. Besides the town council will scream if they have to find money for another hire. I can do just as much as I always could and more if I have to. Don't go making me into an old man. And that's enough of that smelly stuff. My back feels fine now, thank you."

Dave sat up and pulled on his undershirt. He buttoned up the neatly starched and ironed cotton uniform shirt.

"I did a nice job ironing this didn't I?" he asked his wife.

"You did indeed. I was a good teacher." She smiled at him and gave him a kiss on the cheek.

"I never said you are an old man, dear. Just that you aren't as young as you used to be. But, remembering last night, maybe I'll have to change my mind. You acted like a teenager in heat."

"Ah Mary, don't go talking about it. You know I don't like to talk about it. I get all flustered."

Dave's cheeks were burning red and Mary laughed at him and pinched his arm lightly.

"You still blush, Davie. You're really a sweet boy still after all these years. Come down when you're ready and I'll cut you a piece of that chocolate zucchini cake I made last night. By the way, did you ever think that maybe last nights' action might have twitched your back a bit?" With a giggle Mary disappeared down the stairs.

Dave finished dressing, combed his graying hair and thought about the day to come. Holidays were the worst. People would be pouring into Hummingbird Falls for tonight's 9:00 p.m. fireworks. Then the summer tourists would begin their onslaught of the tiny village that lasted through leaf peeping time and then started up again when the cross country, snow boarding and down hill skiing season geared up.

This day he and Colby would walk miles patrolling Main Street in their reflective vests, heavy duty flashlights in hand and gun belts loaded with full gear. It would be a late night, too, by the time all the cars were finally out of town, the hotel bars closed and the late night tourists were safely back in the Inns and Hotels that dotted the mountains surrounding Hummingbird Falls.

Dave sent a special prayer up to the blue sky outside his bedroom window. "Let it be a good holiday for all, Lord. I'm just asking for a little help to keep everything calm and healthy tonight. And please, take care of my back."

49

Then Dave took one last look himself in the mirror and noticed once more that his stomach seemed to be inching its way over the top of his uniform pants. Sighing, he went downstairs to join Mary in a large piece of her prize winning chocolate zucchini cake.

16

The gun shots exploded, sending frightened birds fluttering into the cover of leafy trees and ground creatures scurrying down hiding holes and under brush. Echoes from the shots reverberated against the mountains and rolled into the valley below. Then four more shots burst out, sharp and clear, even closer. Ellie jumped to her feet, her half eaten blueberry turnover tumbling to the porch floor, and ran for the phone to call Dave Shaffer, Chief of Police in Hummingbird Falls. Buddy was barking wildly and running from one end of the porch to the other, not quite sure where the sound was coming from as the sound of the shots bounced from one peak to another much like the rumbles of raucous thunder claps.

Bobby Brady answered the phone with a pleasant, "Hummingbird Falls Police Department. Bobby Brady speaking. How can I help you?"

"Bobby, it's Ellie Hastings, up here on Foster's Brook. I'm being shot at. Someone's blasting off a gun, at least eight shots so far and too close for comfort. It's not hunting season and these woods are posted off limits to hunters. I've got a sweet soft eyed doe nibbling my newly sown grass every evening and I can't stand the thought of her being scared or worse, killed. Where's Dave?"

"Mrs. Hastings, calm down please. Dave's not here right now. I don't want to sound rude, but are you sure you're hearing gun shots? Fire crackers sound a lot like gunshots and after all, it's July 3rd and the fireworks are scheduled to start downtown in a few hours. Maybe some kids are just partying a little early up there with some fire crackers."

"Oh," Ellie said, feeling rather foolish, "that's right. The fireworks are tonight. I forgot. You could be right. But they sure sound like gun shots. I would swear someone's shooting. Sarah called me a few days ago and said she was hearing shots down in town, too."

"Are you hearing the shots now?"

"Well, no. They seem to have stopped."

"Mrs. Hastings, I don't think you have anything to worry about, but please don't feel bad about calling. Several folks downhill from you as well as up your way have called in too, thinking they heard guns going off. But I'd guess it's just fireworks. Do you want me to radio Chief Shaffer?"

"No, I guess not. And anyway, whatever those noises are, I don't hear them anymore. I suppose Dave's out patrolling the road where the fireworks are being set off?"

"Yep, he and Colby are foot patrolling that half mile stretch along the golf course, between Main Street and Route 43 junction, keeping traffic moving, calming down any rowdy high school kids and making sure folks park where they're suppose to."

"Then don't bother him, Bobby. He's pretty busy, I'm sure. But if I hear anymore fire crackers or whatever they are, I'm going to call you back. I don't like people running around in the woods close to my cabin blowing things up, even if it is for the holiday."

"I can understand that, Mrs. Hastings. You be sure and call anytime you want to. But aren't you going down to see the fireworks? I'd go if I could, but I got drafted from the road crew to be dispatcher this year, so I'm stuck here. Everybody'll be there. It's lots of fun."

"Well, now that you've reminded me, I think I will do just that, Bobby. Thank you. And don't bother to tell Dave about my call. I'll see him down there."

"I have to log all calls that I receive. Chief Shaffer reads over the log and decides what he needs to follow up on. So, your call will be listed anyway. And thanks for calling."

Ellie returned to her forest green porch chair rocker, picked up her slightly damaged turnover and finished eating it. Buddy curled up at her feet, and sighed. She'd put off calling Sarah and talking with her about the riddles she'd found in the library and out by Black Bear Bridge. Ellie's mind was still jumping back and forth between believing that the notes were for real and suspecting that someone was teasing her, playing a game that the riddle writer knew she couldn't resist. She decided to wait and see if anything else developed or she received another riddle before she confided in anyone, Sarah or Dave. She didn't want to appear foolish or over reactive. And she still hadn't figured out the crooked heart part of the riddle yet.

Ellie forced her mind to think about more positive events. Just over two weeks ago her son Sandy, his wife Marilyn and her grandson, Joshua, just one month old, disappeared down the curving gravel driveway on their way to the airport and a flight back to their home in Florida. Then Allison, her first born, flew back to her fabulous marketing research job in Columbus, Ohio. They had come to celebrate her early retirement from teaching high school English and the completion of her new log cabin, nestled on twenty acres along Foster's Brook. She missed them already.

Then Ellie took up her pen and started to work on a new poem. She wanted to express her gratitude for all the good things that she had in her life. She worked on the poem for a while, not noticing the time going by until her stomach started its familiar growl.

Ellie looked up through the porch screens to the green woods and then over the tree tops to the view of Mount Adams shimmering in the late afternoon sun. Peaceful quiet had again settled down over the forest. The hummingbirds hovered over the honeysuckle vine that she recently planted on the trellis behind her new perennial garden spot. She heard the happy chickadee-dee-dee call in the pines. The view of the craggy mountains cutting into the brilliant blue of the summer sky never failed to touch her deeply. This late afternoon the sight moved her to tears.

"Thank you, Alice. Without you, this land, this cabin, this peace wouldn't be mine. I'll remember you always. And you, too, Josie."

Everything that happened last year felt like a life time ago. Only the pain from the loss of her two friends still felt new.

With her poem almost completed, the afternoon waning and the peepers beginning their song, Ellie remained content to sit and rock, appreciating the quiet and revisiting the activity filled week that her kids and her dear little grandson shared with her. The retirement party back in the city had been fairly simple but filled with food, of course. Commendations from friends, former students, faculty and staff were glowing and very touching. She was happy her children witnessed the successful closing of this part of her life. The three of them had been through some pretty difficult endings, especially when her husband, Chris, their dad, died from cancer over ten years ago. Saying goodbye to life long friends in the town they'd lived in wasn't easy either. But her kids were grown and ensconced in their own lives and she was already partially established in her new life in the small mountain village of Hummingbird Falls, having summered here the last ten years. With the completion of her new year round home, she was now a full time resident.

They had a lovely week together and now Ellie was alone again. Well, not really alone. She had Buddy. And being alone was fine with her. She had grown accustomed to living on her own, and time to herself was really quite necessary for her poetry writing and painting. But just now, as the large cabin behind her sat vacant and still and the darkness deepened, so did her spirits.

17

"**H**ave you seen Matt?"

"No, Millie. I just this minute got back from hunting for jobs. I haven't really seen Matt since we moved in. Does he still live here?"

"Todd, stop it. He's been here, but I haven't seen him since last night. He's getting up awfully early for him. He used to stay in bed until noon."

"Maybe the country air is good for him."

"I wish I could believe that. He's still so moody and acting downright scary if you ask me. Slouching around here mumbling to himself and never speaking to anyone, not even Michael."

"What do you want me to do? I've been gone the last two days looking for jobs. And, guess what? I found one. I start tomorrow at the Hawks Inn. I'm bartending, 3:00-2:00, eleven hour shift."

Matt forgotten, Millie hugged Todd. "Oh, that's so wonderful. It didn't take you too long. What's your pay?"

Todd frowned. "$8.50 an hour, plus all the tips I get."

"What? $8.50? I don't believe you. You must be kidding. You can't work for that pay. Your shoe shiner in New York made more than that."

"Look Millie, shut up. It's the best I can do right now. They need someone so badly that they didn't even ask for references. We need cash and need it fast. I'll be able to bring home tips every night, plus a paycheck every week. And by the way, they need a hostess and server, too. So you get your butt down there now and see if you can get the job."

"What me? What about the kids? You promised me I'd never have to work a day in my life. And what's a server?"

"A waitress."

"A waitress. Oh no. Oh no. I won't ever be a server and pick up strangers' dirty dishes. How disgusting. It's bad enough around here without a dish washer."

"You said it yourself. We have no choice. Try for the hostess job then."

Millie frowned. "I'll think about it. Maybe if it's a decent place I could dress up a bit and meet some interesting people. At least I'd see someone. I haven't seen anyone since we arrived in this back woods forsaken spot.

"Anyway, I'm glad you're back. And I'm happy you got a job, even though I'll never see you unless I work there too. Maybe that's a good enough reason to work the Inn. At least I'd see you. I'm starved for adults and very sick of kids right now.

Todd started for the porch.

"Wait a moment. Speaking of kids, I want you to find Matt and talk to him about his attitude. And I want you to lay down the law about a job. He's old enough to work and help out a little. Maybe he could wash dishes at the Hawks Inn. That way we could keep an eye on him. Missy's old enough to stay with Michael at night until we get home. She refuses to work and anyway her chances of lining up babysitting or something of that sort is fairly limited, given that no one here knows her."

"Okay. I'll talk to the kid. Where do you think he is?"

"I think he goes off into the woods."

"I'll take a little walk and see if I can find him."

"Before you go, I wanted to tell you about an event that might be fun for us to all go to. Even though it's only the 3rd, there's a 4th of July celebration downtown tonight. I want us to go as a family. Maybe we'll meet some people, make some friends. At the very least if we make an appearance we won't be such strangers."

"I don't know. I don't think we should be so obvious."

"Well, what's more obvious than working as a bar tender or a server?" Miller retorted. "Oh come on, Todd. No one will recognize us and it'll be fun. An old time country celebration with fireworks. It'll be good for the kids and for us too. Just say yes."

"Okay, okay. After I find Matt and after dinner, we'll head down there and try to act as local as we can and try to fit in with the little village people."

Millie laughed. "I don't know if we can look authentic, but we can study these folks and figure out what'll make us look more like we belong. The more we belong the less suspicious we'll be."

"That's true. It's probably a good idea to meet some people and have them get to know us. We won't stand out so much."

Todd kissed Millie on the cheek and smiled at her. She smiled back. It was the first smile either remembered since they moved to Hummingbird Falls. Maybe things were going to work out after all.

Todd walked into the back yard and moved towards the woods. Near the edge he spotted what looked like a well worn path. He pushed the bushes aside and followed the path and slowly he disappeared into the forest.

18

Todd followed the path for about ten minutes before he found the first sign that Matt had been here. A roughly built lean-to made of pine boughs and sticks was set back from the path. In it, Todd saw some canned soup, a can opener, a small pot, some matches in a plastic bag with a paper back book, a small flashlight and a spoon. A couple of bottles of water sat on the ground next to a balled up blanket.

Todd chuckled. The kid was exploring the outdoors for the first time in his life. Matt had never taken to cub scouts or boy scouts, preferring hanging with his friends on the streets or playing video games at other kid's houses. At home in New York, he stayed in his room fooling around on the computer with his earphones blasting music loud enough to injure his eardrums.

The Garibaldi family had never gone camping or taken trips to parks or National Forests. They were strictly a suburban mall oriented group, occasionally flying to resort sites like Walt Disney World, Cancun, or Waikiki, but never getting closer to fresh air than what came out of their purified air conditioned environment.

Matt did a pretty good job building his camping site, even if it was a little rough around the edges. No sign of drugs, cigarettes or liquor, either. That was good.

Todd found the next marker of Matt's activities just a bit further down the trail. What he discovered wasn't so reassuring. In fact, it was absolutely chilling. Several feet off the path was a huge oak tree. High up from the ground a tree limb was wrapped with what looked like a hobo's pack. It was a sheet tied up into a bundle. Todd climbed the tree and pulled the bundle down. He undid the knot. Cursing, he stared at the contents of the sheet. A plastic bag held Todd's shot gun, unused ammunition and casings from about two dozen spent shot gun shells.

Todd tied the sheet back into a bundle and slung it over his back. His kid was up to something no good and he had the proof of it on his back. He was angry and he was worried. What had Matt been up to?

Todd walked on. The trail became steeper and narrower. He passed a sign that read, "You are now entering The White Mountain State Park." Other than the sign, there were no obvious indications where the state park boundaries began. No fence, no stone markers, no gates.

Todd hesitated and then walked on. As the trail wound its way through a growth of young hemlocks, he heard a sound in front of him. Someone else was walking the path, coming his way.

Matt was watching the trail and didn't see his father until Todd called out his name. Matt jumped, startled.

"What are you doing here?" he asked.

"No, the question is, what are you doing here?" his father replied.

"It's a free world. I can go where I want," Matt grumbled.

"Stop it right now. I won't have any of your attitude. Turn around. I want to see where you've been."

"Come on, Dad. I'm just walking. There's nothing down there."

"Down where, Matt? And if there's nothing down there then you don't have to worry, do you?"

Matt looked shaken. "I have nothing to do with it, really Dad. I just found it today."

"Nothing to do with what? I think you and I should just keep on walking from where you came. Let's go."

Reluctantly, Matt turned around and led the way back to where he came from. They walked about a quarter of a mile before Matt stopped.

"I think we'd better keep low from here on," Matt said in a whisper. "You go first, Dad."

Todd bent over and moved slowly ahead. As he rounded a curve in the path he saw where Matt had been and what attracted him. In front of Todd a river was rushing downward. Across the river and all along its banks as far as he can see in the densely wooded area was stretched bright yellow crime scene tape.

19

Todd stood up and looked around. No one was at the crime scene. The only evidence that something very horrible had happened here was the yellow plastic crime tape blowing gently in the breeze.

"Okay. Tell me now. What are you doing out here? And what happened? Why have the police been here?"

"I don't know Dad, really. I was just exploring and I walked down here. I hadn't come so far down this path before. Suddenly, there it was."

"When did you first come here?"

"A couple of days ago, I guess. At first there were lots of people walking around inside that yellow tape. I thought they were cops, so I stayed hidden in the bushes."

"Did anyone see you?"

"No, I don't think so. I didn't see anyone looking my way. They were too busy taking pictures, digging around, looking around the river to notice me. I only stayed a little while because I started to get scared that they'd catch me. So I left."

"Then you came back today?"

"Yeah, I wanted to see what was going on, but no one was here."

"Matt. What are you doing with my gun?"

Matt looked down at his feet. "Nothing."

"Matt. I'm asking you. What were you doing with the shot gun? I found the empty casings. You've shot the gun at least two dozen times. Tell me what you did."

"Geez, nothing, Dad. I shot at a few squirrels and crows. No big deal. I didn't hurt the gun. It's fine."

"I'm not worried about the gun. I'm worried about what you've done. Did you have anything to do with what happened down there? I want the truth. It'll come out anyway. So tell me. Did you shoot the gun down there?"

"What the hell do you think I am? A murderer? A fool? A stupid kid? I'm your son. I'm not some thrill killer. I only shot at some dumb animals and birds. I wouldn't shoot at a person."

"A person was killed down there? How do you know?"

"I overheard one of the cops say something about it's a lonely place to die. So I assumed someone died."

"Who died, Matt?"

"I don't know Dad. I'm telling you I had nothing to do with it. Why don't you believe me? Can't you pay attention to what I'm telling you for once? I'm not lying. I'm your kid. Don't you know that I wouldn't do anything like that?"

Matt broke down in tears and turned around and started hiking back up the trail toward home. Todd reached out as Matt passed him, but Matt stepped out of the way to avoid his father's touch. Todd shrugged his shoulders, shook his head in bewilderment and slowly followed his boy up the trail.

20

Dave picked up the phone.
"Dave Shaffer, Chief of Hummingbird Fall's Police Department. What can I do for you?"

"Dave, it's Bill Crandall, SBI. How're you doing? Haven't seen you in a while. Are the moose keeping you busy up there?"

"Hi Bill. Good to hear from you. Yep, we're mobbed by moose and transported with tourists. Big fireworks' night in the village. And we're being run ragged."

"I forgot you hold your fireworks early. But I remember you get quite a crowd for the festivities. Must keep you pretty busy."

"Yep, you're lucky to get me in. Just stopped to deputize a couple of the local guys to help us out tonight, but I'm finally beginning to realize we need more man power in this little village. Why don't you come on down and help us out and enjoy the fireworks with us at the same time?"

"Thanks for the invite, Dave, but I'm up to my ears in an investigation. But I've got an idea that might work for you. There's a new recruit who just finished Cop Academy and with some of the highest scores, too. She's a local gal. In fact, she's the daughter of one of my SBI buddies, so I know she's got cop in her blood and she's grown up around the field. She's looking for a part time job for the summer that'll give her some training until she finds a full time job in the fall. Why don't I send her down for a trial?"

"Hmm, I don't know, Bill. I haven't got time to train someone new today."

"Hey, she can direct traffic or patrol the streets tonight. She doesn't need any extra training for that and you can get a take on her. I'll explain to her that it's just for tonight and maybe a few more days. That way she won't have any expectations. Then if you think she'll work out you can hire her for the summer."

"I don't know. This's pretty sudden, but I sure could use an extra hand tonight. What's her name?"

"Rosie O'Rourke. Big strapping Irish lass. Her Dad says she can beat him arm wrestling and at just about everything else, including shooting, so she must be good."

"Well, I don't usually make snap decisions, but I do have some extra money for temps for this weekend, so send her on down. She needs to fill out the paper work and I'd like to talk with her a little bit before things get too busy. Can she be here in an hour or so?"

"Tell you what. I'll call her and give her your number. You can take it from there. Hope it helps you out."

"Thanks, Bill. Your call certainly comes at a great time."

"Well, that brings me back to why I'm calling you. You might not be so happy hearing what I'm going to tell you. I want to give you a heads up on something that's going on."

"Oh? Must be top secret. I haven't seen anything exciting in the papers lately."

"Well, the vic is a Jane Doe right now, so we haven't released any information to the press. I wanted to call you because the body was found in the White Mountain State Park, near the boundary with Hummingbird Falls. Actually, another mile and this case would've been yours instead of mine. She was found right where the Crooked River splits, opposite Crooked Heart Island."

"I know the place. Thank God for boundaries that put the body on your side and not mine. What happened?"

"Homicide. White female, 30-40's, no id. Shot in the back and left in a stream. Cause of death, two of the nine buck shot in her back made it to her heart. She bled out. Cold water kept her pretty well preserved. The weapon's a shot gun. We recovered the nine shot that penetrated but no sign of the gun."

"Could it have been an accident? Even though it's not hunting season, some folks do go out practice shooting. Kids sometimes shoot at one thing and hit another. How do you know she was murdered?"

"Well, the ME found some bruises on the body, some indication on the wrists that restraints were used. Enough so he's decided it's a homicide."

"Anything found on site?"

"Nope, not yet. We're going over it with a fine tooth comb, believe me. Rain washed out a lot. I just wanted you to know about it in case anything unusual happens in your area, suspicious characters, missing persons, that sort of thing."

"Haven't had any missing persons reports, but there are lots of strangers coming in for the fireworks. Come to think of it, we've had several complaints about shooting in the woods and near the village, but no one has been hurt that I've heard of and up until now I've chocked it up to kids with fire cracker spirit."

"When was the shooting heard? Do you have any time frames?"

"Not off hand. The dispatcher took most of the calls. We haven't really treated it all that seriously. Just thought it was kids with firecrackers scaring the locals."

"Would you look into it a bit more for me, Dave, when you get a chance? Maybe you could put Rosie on it if she works out."

"I'd be glad to, Bill. Could be there really was someone shooting around here and if so, maybe our shootings are connected to your case. I'll get a list of the people who complained about hearing gun shots and tomorrow I'll try to follow up with some of them, or have Colby or maybe Rosie, if she works out tonight. I'll keep an ear out and have Colby talk to some of his contacts to see if they know anything."

"That would be a great help, thanks. How's that kid doing? He's been working for you for what, two years now?"

"Yep, going on three. After some attitude adjustments and reality checks, he's doing just fine. Still delighting the ladies. But he's going to be a top cop as time goes on. He has the instinct and the nature. I'm proud of him. Thanks for asking."

"Well, you saved him from a possible life of crime and turned him into someone fighting crime, a double score. You deserve credit for that."

"Thanks, Bill. If I can help out on that homicide in any way be sure to call. And while you're so close to town, please come and sample some of Mary's cooking. We'd love to see you."

"Thanks. Will do when I get a minute. I'll keep you posted. Have a great holiday."

"Oh, and thanks for Rosie O'Rourke. I'll let you know how that works out."

Dave hung up the phone. He and Bill Crandall went back years to when they were both enrolled in the Police Academy in Concord. Dave was glad to hear from him. But news of a murder in the State Park was not good. Dave didn't like the thought of a killer wandering around in his territory. Or the possibility that one of his own villagers might be the victim or, perhaps, the murderer.

21

Ellie wasn't going to let the dark stillness or threatening riddles that just might be giant hoaxes bring her down. She jumped up from her porch chair and gathered up her folding chair, bug spray, a bottle of water, and her purse and car keys. She tucked a small left over raspberry scone into a plastic bag and put it in her pocket, leashed up Buddy and drove down the mountain road, past the falls and into town.

"Another wonderful thing about living in Hummingbird Falls," Ellie told Buddy who was watching and listening to her intently as usual, "is that we never have to be alone. There are 800 wonderful souls, most of whom would be happy to chat or share a hello with us, whenever we need to hear another voice. And so, that's where we're going tonight. We'll see the fireworks with our neighbors and friends and have fun, too."

She pulled her Subaru into the back of the line of cars edging into the golf course parking lot and found one of the last spaces left. Next to her were two white vans that looked familiar. The logo on the side of the vans read FOSTER HOME FOR CHILDREN. She was happy that James Foster and his staff brought their kids into town for the festivities. Ellie hoped she would run into him. She usually saw him on Friday's, the day she ran the library's tutoring group for those children at the home who could benefit from some extra help in reading. Sometimes she saw James' kids at the library on Tuesday's when the children's reading club met. She'll keep an eye out for James and his group tonight.

Since James returned to Hummingbird Falls last year after his half-sister Alice's murder, he had slowly reintegrated into his old home town and renewed friendships with people he had known all of his life before he fled thirteen years ago, afraid of being accused of the murder of his girl friend and her parents. With his name cleared and a large inheritance from his sister, he renovated the family mansion into a home for children who have been orphaned or traumatized.

The reputation of The Foster Home for Children had steadily grown under his direction. James had expanded services and now offered an outpatient facility for troubled youth as well as a residential home for children who needed therapy before adoption was possible.

Ellie and James had become good friends over the year. They often ate dinner together and James had come to depend on Ellie's experience as an educator and consulted with her on some of his more difficult cases. At times, over the candlelight dinners, while sharing a warm brandy in front of a crackling fire, a thought would whisper in Ellie's mind about how nice it had been when she and her husband Chris had snuggled before a cozy fireplace on a cold winter night. But that was many years ago and a dim memory now. She and James had grown close, but as yet they had not struck the match that could set the kindling inside them afire.

But Ellie hoped she would see James at the festivities tonight. Maybe she could join their group.

Quite a crowd had already gathered and the fireworks were still almost thirty minutes away from starting. She unloaded her chair, put the bug spray in one pocket, her water bottle in the other with the raspberry scone, and led Buddy out of the parking lot to the street which streamed with people walking about. Patriotic band music blared out of speakers set up on the Golf Club steps. An ice cream push cart, pop corn stand, helium balloon vender, the pie lady and The Historical Society soft drink and cookie booth lined the curb, advertising that 10% of all profits will go to the American Veterans Association. As she tried to decide if she should support the Veterans by buying some ice cream, pop corn, pie and a root beer, Danny Collins thrust a miniature American flag in her hand.

"Happy fourth, Ellie. Flag is free, compliments of the Kiwanis. Keep on waving the red, white and blue."

"Thanks Danny. You must have bought a bunch. Everyone seems to have one. All those waving flags look pretty and very patriotic. I'm trying to decide where to park myself. Where's the best place to see the fireworks going off?"

"Practically anywhere on this stretch of road has a great view. No tall trees to obstruct the full display and if you sit up on that slope over there you can see even if people get in front of you. Fireworks are on the third tee."

He pointed across the street to the overflow golf course parking lot that sat back from the road and was partially hidden by young bushy cedar trees. In front of the trees a grassy area sloped gradually down to the side walk.

"Lots of folks are over there on that little hill in front of the parking spaces. That's close to the food, has a perfect view across the street to the third tee. Plus you can see everyone as they walk by so you won't miss a thing."

"Sounds good to me, Danny. Thanks for the flag."

Ellie crossed the street and cars going both ways stopped for her and Buddy and for several other people as well and waved them across smiling. Jaywalkers had the right of way in this village. She found a perfect spot up high on the slope, but close enough to the edge so she could escape quickly if Buddy or she needed to find a bathroom or scout out the food venders some more. Ellie opened up her folding chair and placed it near but not too close to a large blanket convention hunkered down on her right next to the parking lot driveway. Four blankets were drawn together forming a huge square and were loaded with picnic baskets and coolers, kids of all ages, including several babies, and hula hoops, soccer balls, sparklers, dolls, stuffed animals and mounds of crinkly cellophane bags of every kind of chip Ellie ever heard of. Several families claimed the space and at least fifteen children all under the age of ten were rolling around, screaming, jumping, wrestling, playing hide and seek and begging for ice cream, food and drink from the assorted group of adults they belonged to. The group of parents was gathered at one end of the blankets, occasionally yelling out directions, warnings or scoldings to the masses of kids as they ran wildly to and fro.

Ellie recognized two of the women as Jean and Alma. Evidently, they had gathered up their kids and joined with some other families to enjoy the holiday together. They certainly seemed to be having a boisterous and fun time. Ellie waved hello to Jean and Alma, but smiled and shook her head no when they waved for her to come over. She didn't think she and Buddy would enjoy being in the center of all that bustle.

Ellie called, "Thank you. I'll stop over later." The women yelled back, "Okay."

On Ellie's other side a family group was lined up in folding chairs. She didn't know them and suspected they were tourists by their fashionable and spotless attire. The mother and father of the family looked tired and seemed to be quietly arguing with each other. They were too far away for her to hear what they were saying, but it was obvious that they were not having a good time. The three kids, two boys and a girl, didn't look like any Hummingbird Falls children she knew. The teenage boy was dressed in oversized hip hop fashion, complete with a reversed cap and diamond studs in his ears. The pre-teen aged girl looked like she was dressed for a prom. Strapless satin tightly accentuated her small breasts and skin tight jeans encircled by a studded belt led Ellie's eye to her gold thong high heel sandals. The youngest boy was dressed in baggy shorts that fell almost to his ankles and a t-shirt that advertised Twisted Truth, a euro rock band. The three children were picking and kicking at each other while slumped down in their seats. Every once in a while one of them pointed out somebody walking by and whispered and then the three of them would burst out laughing very loudly. Several other people around this group had moved their blankets and chairs further away. They were not a fun group to be around.

Buddy gave them a look and shook his head as if wondering what people were coming to these days and then cooperated by lying down right away and close to Ellie's feet, watching with her as the crowd grew larger and louder. Talking had escalated into yelling in an attempt to be heard above the huge speakers belting out John Phillips Souza band music and other patriotic tunes.

A teenage boy was working the crowd and as he approached Ellie Buddy started to growl.

"He won't hurt you. He's just protecting me," Ellie said as loudly as she could. She didn't like yelling, but in this delightful chaos it was yell or forget about communicating at all.

The young man took a step closer and held his hand out to Buddy. Buddy returned the favor by licking the boy's hand thoroughly and satisfied that this kid was safe, lay down again. The boy wiped his hand on his pants and then held up his wares. Ellie could see the red, white and blue glow sticks in his hand.

"Two for five dollars. Proceeds go to the vets. The sticks fit together into a circle. Lots of folks are putting them around their kid's necks so when it gets really dark they can still spot them. Want two for your dog? He'll look great and you can keep track of him if he gets loose."

She laughed. "You sold me, young man. I'll take two for five dollars."

The vender cracked the sticks and the color flowed down, illuminating them.

"They'll look even better when it's dark," he said as he took Ellie's money and moved on to the next group.

Ellie fixed the glow sticks into circles and gently pulled them over Buddy's head.

"You look just fine, Buddy, very American," Ellie said as Buddy shook his head a couple of times before lying back down. "And I don't have to worry if you stray off in the dark, because the glow sticks will tell me just where you are and what you're up to."

22

Ellie settled down too and started one of her favorite occupations, people watching. The festive crowd supplied many entertaining characters and she was fascinated at the wide array of fashion, if one could call little strips of cotton across young girls' chests and itsy bitsy shorts, fashionable. But then, old t-shirts with beer ads or inappropriate slogans, droopy jeans and shorts down to the calf weren't especially appealing to her either.

She was surprised that so many people were strangers. Tourists accounted for some of the unknown people, but so many families with herds of little children trooped by that she wondered if the neighboring towns were invading Hummingbird Falls tonight for a preview of the bigger fireworks displays that would be popping down Route 43 in Greenberg tomorrow night.

Ellie searched for familiar faces among the mob, but other than spotting several of the inn owners that she'd met over the years she didn't see anyone she knew. She wondered where her friends Margaret, Sarah, Mary Shaffer, Debbie and Bonnie were.

They wouldn't miss this event, she was sure. She should have thought to call them to connect before she left. But then again, it was so noisy that she wouldn't have been able to hear them chat anyway and she wasn't in the mood to have to yell every time she wanted to say anything. She hadn't seen James or his staff and children either. They must be off in a more secluded area where the racket was less overwhelming. She decided that she was perfectly happy sitting in the middle of all this cheerful chaos by herself.

It was a Norman Rockwell painting. Flags waved, music blared, children and dogs scrambled here and there. People were slurping ice cream, crunching pop corn, downing soda and water in the warm summer night. Across the darkening golf course, fireflies flickered. Dave Shaffer, Chief of Police, and Colby Conners, his handsome young assistant, wearing bright reflective vests and carrying large flashlights, were walking up and down the packed street in opposite directions, greeting folks, patting kids' and dogs' heads, directing traffic and working the crowd like politicians. Ellie saw several other folks, Mike, Reggie, Larry and John Jenkins with reflective vests also. She figured they were helping out with the traffic tonight.

She also spotted a woman she had never seen before in full police gear. Reflective vest, official uniform, heavy gun loaded belt, night stick, black boots and regulation head gear didn't hide the bright red hair braided and hanging half way down her back. She was tall and attractive, and obviously in great shape. She looked like she knew what she was doing as she signaled cars where to turn, when to stop, or move ahead with her theatrically exaggerated hand gestures, whistles, and body language. She was putting on quite a show and many who were assembled waiting for the fire works clapped as she whirled around to point at the stopped traffic and waved them on with a bow. She danced on the asphalt, coordinating her arms and body gracefully and with skill.

Cars continued to pour down the road and as the time for the fireworks approached, latecomers were having a difficult time finding a spot to park. Headlights spotlighted the woman directing traffic as she skillfully sent them down to parking areas further away from the crowded site where Ellie sat waiting.

The blanket family group next to her continued to noisily ebb and flow with children as they ran off on some fun venture and returned only to take off again. The older children reigned in toddlers while Jean and Alma and the other parents chatted and laughed. Three and four year olds played a kind of tag and run, darting out of sight and then reappearing behind the large cedar bushes that lined the parking lot. Everyone seemed to be having a wonderful time and Ellie was glad she'd come. Every once in a while fire crackers were set off, spooking the crowd, making Buddy and Ellie jump and reminding her of the loud noises she heard in the woods earlier at home. The firecrackers did sound a lot like gun shots.

She noticed several other singles among this predominately family gathering. One young pigtailed woman was sitting cross legged on a towel, reading a paperback novel and paying no attention to her surroundings. She spotted an older woman sitting on a folding chair like hers. She was wrapped up in a long sweater, even though the weather was warm and muggy. Her cane leaned against her knees and she was smiling at a bunch of little boys who were trying to stand on their heads. A man stood alone near the cedar bushes, holding a blanket. He didn't seem very happy. His eyes were flitting over the crowd, darting here and there, and his mouth turned down at the corners as if he had eaten something that didn't agree with him.

Something about him just wasn't right. Through the dusk Ellie studied his face, scarred and pale, like his skin had never been touched by the sun. His eyes were dark and small and constantly moving. His black hair was combed straight back from his face; his broad forehead shone with sweat. He was tall and looked to be in very good shape for a forty something man. Despite the warm weather, he was dressed in long pants and a long sleeved shirt, both black.

Ellie glanced away and then looked back at the man once more. She felt anxiety trickle down her neck and inch up her spine. She didn't like this man, not one bit, and he frightened her in a way she could not describe. Could he be the one who left the note in the library? Did he leave the cup and saucer at Black Bear Bridge? Was he the one who was warning her that she had to solve the mystery or be sorry? Whoever he was, she wished he would just disappear.

Buddy growled softly deep in his throat and Ellie bent over and reassured him, patting his head and whispering sweet nothings in his ear. When she looked up again, she found she had received her wish. The strange man was gone.

23

Ellie put the thought of the strange man out of her mind and turned back to the festivities around her. She was content to be alone within this happy crowd, a part of something bigger than herself and in the town where she now belonged.

A chatter of children roused her attention. Three young girls about four or five, blond hair hanging freely down their backs, little summer sun dresses barely covering their browned summer skin, glow stick halos circling their heads, had strayed too far with their game of hide and seek. With darkness descending Jean sent an older sister to bring the girls back to the blanket area and they were protesting with little yelps and resisting, trying to escape their sister's hands.

The evening had turned from dusk to early dark, with just the first stars popping out and no moon to cast light over the crowd. The three Hummingbird Falls' lamp posts located over the half mile of this part of Main Street were far apart and their little circles of light didn't reach very far.

Just as the older sister grabbed the fabric of two of the girls' sundresses and pulled them toward the blanket, a large boom exploded and the crowd erupted with cries of anticipation, every eye staring up at the dark sky. A burst of red, white and blue stars spread across the heavens and twirled on its way toward the earth. A huge boom announced its demise as another red rocket immediately streamed noisily upward, ready to surprise the already mesmerized crowd with its gift of glittery ooh and ahh inspiring spectacular explosions.

The next half hour was amazing, filled with huge discharges of fireworks that would challenge even Gandalf the Great to match. Buddy didn't mind the noise half as much as some of the little children did. Clutching their ears they clung to their parents and screamed, half fearfully, half with excitement, waiting for the next sky dance display.

The finale almost did Ellie in. Her neck ached from being bent at such an awkward angle, but she didn't dare move it in case she missed even one bit of the spectacular show above. The series of booms and sprays of light and color delighted her. She was totally caught in the moment of July Fourth delight, sore neck and all. And now she understood why so many people were laying flat down. They didn't have to deal with sore necks. She made a mental note to bring a blanket next year.

The applause and cheers from the crowd after the last rocket fizzled to the ground almost drowned out the frantic voice calling, "Carrie, Carrie. Oh God, where is Carrie?"

Ellie glanced first at the small family group sitting beside her, confused about where the cries were coming from. The mother and father were folding up their chairs. The girl and little boy were looking around.

"Where's Matt?" the mother asked.

The children shrugged their shoulders.

"He's gone," Missy said. "He got up a little while ago. I asked him where he was going and he didn't answer."

Todd and Millie looked around. People were in motion everywhere: children ran in and out, adults folded blankets and chairs, traffic started to turn onto and filled the narrow street.

"We'll never find him in this mess," Todd said. "I should have handcuffed him to me. I should have known he'd pull something like this."

"Something like what?" Missy asked. "What's he done now, Dad?"

"Never mind. Let's get out of here."

"But what about Matt?" Michael whined.

"He knows the way back to the car. He's probably there waiting for us," Millie said. "Before we panic, let's go back to the car."

Ellie watched them pack up and walk down the slope. She wondered who they were and what their son Matt, the one with the diamonds in his ears, was up to.

Then she heard the shrieking voice again. She turned around to look at the blanket family beside her. Jean was wringing her hands, a terrified look on her face. A man herded the children into a circle in the center of the blanket and told them to stay there and not move. Alma and two men started calling "Carrie, Carrie, where are you?" as they moved away from the blanket, apparently searching for a lost child.

Ellie could see how easy it would be for a child to get lost on a night like this. The bustling crowd, the joyful freedom the children experienced as they ran about, the atmosphere of safety that hovered over Hummingbird Falls would reassure any parent enough so they might let their vigilance relax. And in the wink of a minute, a little girl was gone.

A crowd started to form around the frantic mother as she broke into loud wails of fear.

24

Dave Shaffer came running up. "What's the problem?" he asked.

"My little girl, Carrie, is missing. She was right here and now she's gone," Jean sobbed.

"Did any of you see her leave?" Dave questioned the children clustered together on the blanket. They looked terrified. They shook their heads no.

One girl, tears running down her cheeks said, "Mom sent me to get the girls and bring them back when the fireworks started. I thought Carrie was with us."

"Give me a description of Carrie, what she is wearing, please," Dave demanded of the crying mother.

"She has on a pink sundress and pink flip flops. She has long blond hair. She's little. She's only four." Jean broke down in tears again.

Dave quickly gathered a party of men and women who were standing around and formed them into teams of two. He directed each team to search a specific area in the vicinity of the family's blanket. The searchers disappeared, calling out Carrie's name as they looked under bushes and parked cars. It was very dark away from the street area and finding a little girl wasn't going to be easy.

Ellie walked over to Dave. "I don't know if this is important or if it means anything, but I saw someone."

"Get on with it Ellie. I'm busy now," Dave said as he moved briskly to another group of onlookers.

"You people. Divide in teams of two. I want each team to go across the street and search the golf course. Each team pick a different tee and walk the hole. Then report back. We're looking for a little four year old girl named Carrie with long blond hair, dressed in pink."

Ellie tapped Dave on the shoulder. "I saw a man, back there, near where the little girls were playing. I thought he looked weird, out of place. Maybe he took her."

"Ellie. Did you see him take her?"

"No, but…"

"Did you see him do anything that would be called suspicious?"

"Well, he was alone. He was dressed all in black. He had a blanket."

"Ellie, don't waste my time. We're looking for a lost kid. What you've told me doesn't relate."

"What can I do, then, Dave?" Ellie asked.

"Ellie, why don't you take Buddy back to the kid's blanket and give him a good smell of something that she might have touched? I know he isn't a trained search and rescue dog, but until Mike gets his bloodhound down here, maybe Buddy could give it a try."

Buddy looked eager, so Ellie walked back to Carrie's blanket and kneeled down. She lifted a corner of the blanket to Buddy's nose and rubbed his face gently with it. One of the children crawled over and handed her a fuzzy teddy bear.

"That's Carrie's bear. Maybe it smells like her," the little boy said.

Buddy liked the smell of the teddy. He sniffed and snuffed and started to lick one corner of the bear's ear.

Ellie pulled Buddy up and carrying the teddy bear with her, she said, "OK Buddy, find Carrie. Where is she?"

Buddy looked up at her. He seemed a little confused.

Ellie urged him on. She stuck the teddy bear under his nose. "Go on Buddy. Go. Find Carrie." She waved her hand in the direction of the darkness away from the blanket.

Buddy took a few steps away. He put his nose to the ground. He wagged his tail and took a few more steps.

Ellie continued to encourage him, gave him smells of the teddy bear whenever he stopped and praised him for every step he took. Buddy finally seemed to get the idea. He took a few steps and then looked back at her. Ellie loaded him with compliments and he took a few more steps away and stopped again to look at her. Ellie didn't know if they were making any progress or not, but she was willing to let Buddy try as long as he was doing something. Ellie wasn't one for just sitting around when action needed to be taken. Better to do something than nothing was one of her mottos.

After a few minutes Buddy and Ellie were out of the parking lot and wandering in the meadow that lined the back nine of the golf course. Buddy was very intent now, following some scent he picked up. Ellie stumbled behind him in the dark, hoping he knew what he was doing, and gave little cries of encouragement.

Suddenly Buddy started to pull at the leash and run, nose to the ground. Ellie tried to keep up with him, but she couldn't see where they were going and had to tug him to a slower pace to keep her footing. He headed deeper into the meadow. Ellie started calling, "Carrie, Carrie, are you here? Where are you?"

Then Buddy stopped and started to scratch at the ground, growling. Ellie caught up to him and bent down. The dim light from the stars made it very hard to see and she didn't have her flashlight. She leaned lower and felt around her, close to where Buddy was growling and digging. The ground was damp with early dew and she felt something wet around a small area that had been cleared in the tall grass. Suddenly her hand dipped into a hole. She yanked her hand out fast and jumped to her feet, scared to death. She forced herself to breathe deeply three times and then bent over again to look at what Buddy had found.

25

Ellie peered down, straining to see what the dark was hiding. She gently pulled Buddy back so she could see what he was digging at. And what Buddy had found clearly was not a little girl, nor a burial site. It was a groundhog's hole. He had followed a groundhog's scent all this way.

Ellie stood up very disappointed and at the same time very relieved. She patted Buddy's head. "That's all right boy. You did your best. After all, you've never had any practice or lessons and you did trail something. You did good, boy."

They turned around and headed back toward the crowd on Main Street. The lights that illuminated the parking lot area from where they had started seemed far away. Ellie was sad that they hadn't uncovered any clues or found the little girl, but she was really glad that her worst fears about what Buddy might have found had not been realized.

As they came nearer to Main Street Ellie noticed that a large crowd was now gathered around Carrie's blanket. As she made her way closer and peeked around bodies and over shorter heads, she saw a scene she'd never forget. Jean, weeping, was sitting on the blanket clutching an adorable blond haired girl to her chest who was wearing a pink dress and pink flip flops. The little girl was crying too. A man who she guessed was Jean's husband, Van, was hugging them both. Dave was quietly talking to them and their companions. The group of other children were smiling and wiggling around in the center of the blanket, hugging and kissing one another joyfully.

Dave turned around and faced the crowd. "OK folks, thanks for your concern and help, but everything has turned out just fine. Seems Carrie got a little turned around in the dark and wandered off. She was found just a little way from here, lost and scared, but she's just fine. So, let's get the traffic moving and get home to our beds. Happy Fourth to you all."

Dave turned back to the family on the blanket as the crowd broke up slowly and headed down the street or back to their cars. Ellie saw Mike telling Reggie to let the cars proceed and then Mike headed back up the street to the junction of Route 4 and 19 to inform Colby and the new red haired officer that the search was called off. Traffic could move again without restriction. The crisis was over.

Ellie sank down in her folding chair which was still sitting just where she left it, with her purse underneath untouched.

"That's Hummingbird Falls," Ellie whispered to Buddy. "I can leave my money and belongings right out on a busy street unattended and trust that no one will take them. And little girls are not stolen here in Hummingbird Falls. They just get lost once in a while."

The pie lady passed by. "Ellie, I have two pieces of three berry pie left. Bargain rates. Can I tempt you?"

"Are the stars shining in Hummingbird Falls?" Ellie answered. "Only two pieces left? I'll take a whole pie, if you have it."

"Sorry, only two pieces left. Here, they're all wrapped up. Only $4.00. That's a dollar off. We did really well tonight. The Vets will be getting a nice contribution."

Ellie dug in her purse. She pulled out a five. "Keep the change. Your pies should never be marked down. Especially the three berry ones. Ummm. Blueberry's my favorite. Strawberry's my next favorite. And raspberry's my next to next favorite. And I've got them all in one. It's a fine night."

This evening was turning back into the Norman Rockwell picture again. All Ellie needed was a pint of vanilla ice cream from the deli to top her pie and Buddy and she could head back to their beautiful new cabin satisfied with the promise of a happy ending for tonight.

"That's Hummingbird Falls," Ellie said to Buddy as they walked to the car. "Full of happy endings."

When they arrived at the car, Ellie saw an envelope underneath her windshield wipers. She took it out and stared at the writing on the front of the envelope. In printed block letters, it read:

READ IMMEDIATELY

"Uh oh, another one. Get in the car Buddy, quick."

Ellie unlocked the car door and she and Buddy hopped in. Ellie locked the doors and looked around. Most of the crowd had left and there were only a few cars remaining in the dark parking lot. She saw a few families still strolling about, probably heading for their cars and home, but she didn't see the man in black or anyone who looked menacing.

She tore open the envelope. A message stared at her, written in large block letters.

I SAW YOU ENJOY YOURSELF TONIGHT. YOU GOT PIE WHILE TIME RAN BY. BETTER HURRY LIKE THE

RIVER RUNS AND WHERE IT SPLITS THE NEXT
CLUE SITS. THE CROOKED HEART WAITS FOR YOU
WITH YET ANOTHER CLUE.

26

Ellie spent hours reading the riddles, and studying the map of Hummingbird Falls, trying to figure out where Crooked Heart was. She worried if she should be taking the warnings in the notes seriously or not. Was someone just playing with her, knowing she was a sucker for mysteries? Was the note writer telling the truth and planning something dangerous or bizarre? What was the riddler's motivation? The riddler hadn't named a particular outcome or punishment, only made reference that the reader of the notes was going to be sorry if she didn't solve the puzzle. And was Crooked Heart a place, a person or a thing? Was it some kind of word code she had to figure out or was it the name of some boutique or gift shop? She didn't know. And the reference to the river and where it split? All the rivers she knew in this area split up into side creeks and brooks dozens of times. She couldn't possibly check them all out. The note writer warned that she better hurry. Why the emphasis on time? What was going to happen and when and to whom?

Ellie decided that she must get another opinion as soon as she could. It was too late tonight to call anyone, except the police. She didn't want to involve Dave and launch a police investigation until someone else judged that these notes and riddles were more than a well planned trick. She needed to find some proof that the note writer really meant what he said. Sarah would be just the one to talk to. Ellie wished now she had talked with Sarah earlier. Sarah would help Ellie decide what to do, but she couldn't call her this late. She'd call first thing in the morning.

27

Sarah beat her to it. The phone rang six times before Ellie could find it and put the right end to her ear.

"Hello?" she mumbled.

Sarah was sputtering on the phone again. "I was awake all night. Someone's shooting off guns all over town. I called Dave last night and he said he's fielded calls from seven people about the gun shots. He said he'd look into it, but he believes it's only people celebrating the fourth, shooting off fireworks. Of course, he can't explain the buckshot that Officer O'Rourke dug out of my back wall. She said they were shotgun pellets, commonly known as buck shot. Dave tried to tell me that they've probably been in my wall for years and I just noticed it now because I'm all in a dither. Now I've lived in this village a long time and this kind of craziness has never happened before. I think something bad's going on and I'll find out myself what's happening if Dave and that police department don't want to."

Ellie wasn't even out of bed yet. Sarah had called her at 6:00 a.m. just as she was dreaming about beautiful gardens filled with tea cups that were chasing hearts around in a kind of Alice in Wonderland way.

"Say that again, Sarah. I'm not quite awake yet."

"Oops, sorry, didn't mean to wake you. I'm used to getting up this early 'cause I usually have to be at the Post Office by 7 a.m., as you know, to bring in mail bags and raise the flag. Today being the Fourth of July, an official Federal holiday, the Post

Office's closed. I don't have to work and sorry, I forgot you don't have to work either."

"What's happening? Shots? Is anyone hurt?"

"Not that I know of. Dave keeps saying it's most likely only firecrackers left over from last night or kids celebrating the fourth until they run out of noise makers. But I don't believe him. I'm old enough to tell a gun shot from a fire cracker. And I told him so too. And Rosie O'Rourke told him about the buck shot she pulled out of my wall."

"What'd he say then? And who is Rosie O'Rourke?"

"The usual. He'd look into it. Nice way of dismissing me. What I'm calling you for is to see if you've heard any more guns shooting up your way. And to answer your other question, Rosie O'Rourke's a very nice young woman who listened very intensely to what I had to say. She's a gift to this police force. That's who she is."

"You mean they're hiring a new police officer?"

"I don't know about hiring. She's working the fourth of July because they're so busy. Larry couldn't make it to my house because of some road problem, so they sent Rosie. She told me she's new, only just been hired an hour before she came to my house. I'll tell you what though. They should hire her permanently. She listens very well. Anyway, back to the point, did you hear any gun shots?"

"Matter of fact, Sarah, early last night before the fireworks, I heard some shots and then after the fireworks, coming back home, I thought I heard some more. But Bobby Brady convinced me they were only fire crackers. That must be the police line. They sure sounded like gun shots to me, too. But, to be honest, last night the fire crackers going off at the fireworks did sound like gunshots. I don't know if I could tell the difference."

"Well, I think they're gun shots. What should we do, Ellie? If someone's shooting at all hours, then something's going on. I don't like it."

"Me either," Ellie agreed. "Look, just give me a minute to get up, brush my teeth and call Mike. He's just down the road. I'll see if he's heard anything. He gets around. If anyone's talking, he'd know about it."

"You do that and give me a call back. You and I will look into this ourselves. Forget those police. We'll do just what we did last summer. We'll investigate, follow the clues and figure it out. Then Dave and Colby can clean it up."

"Sarah, we got into trouble doing that before, if you remember. Now, I'll call Mike and let you know what he says. Then, we'll take it from there. If he heard shots too, maybe he has some idea where they came from or who might be shooting. Then we can decide what to do. If he didn't hear anything weird, then maybe that will just be the end of it."

"I'm betting he heard shots, Ellie. Maybe he can join up with us. We could use a man if we're going to sneak around in the woods at night, looking for the shooter."

"Sarah, stop right there. We're not running around in any woods at night when there's shooting. We'd get ourselves killed. What can you be thinking of?"

"I'm thinking of stopping that shooting before anyone gets killed, Ellie. None of us are safe with bullets zooming all around us. This is our village and if our police won't take care of it, then we'll do it ourselves. That's the right of every citizen and I take that responsibility seriously. I have to. After all, I am a government employee."

"Okay, okay, Sarah. Give me a few minutes and I'll call Mike and then get back to you."

Ellie thought for a second about her decision to confide in Sarah about her own problem with the threatening riddles she received, but decided against revealing this information for now. She'd take care of Sarah's request first and then when she called her back she'd set up a meeting with her. Then she could show Sarah the riddles and the cup and saucer and talk with her face to face about what to do.

Ellie said goodbye, hung up the phone and crawled out of bed. She dressed and let Buddy out to do his morning routine. She knew she couldn't call Mike before her own morning routine was completed, so she put on a pot of coffee and got out the last piece of three berry pie. She had just finished her second cup of coffee and was devouring the last bite of the pie when her phone rang again. It was Dave.

"I need to talk to you, Ellie. I'm on my way. Be there in three minutes."

Ellie stammered, "OK, Dave. What's up? Are you OK?"

"No," was his answer. "I'll talk to you when I get there." Now what?

Ellie poured Dave's coffee, and left it black, the only way he would tolerate it, when he pulled the big black Hummingbird Falls patrol SUV into the parking space out front. She opened the door for him and followed him through the kitchen where he picked up his coffee and on out to the screen porch where he made himself at home on the rattan love seat. He took two good gulps of the steaming coffee.

"Good. You always know how to make a good cup of coffee, just like Mary. Strong, not bitter."

Ellie waited before saying anything. Patience was not one of her virtues, but she promised herself to practice it as long as she could, especially when dealing with Dave who had little tolerance for impulsive behavior or interruptions. Today she sensed she'd be better served with silent attention then with her usual barrage of questions she was accustomed to throwing out in her quest to satisfy her unending curiosity.

Dave finished his coffee and walked back into the kitchen and poured himself another cup. He returned slowly back to the porch and stood looking over the woods.

"This's a two or three cup of coffee situation."

Ellie bite her tongue and waited.

"Last night didn't turn out quite as well as I expected."

That was just too much. Ellie burst out, patience tossed and brain firing.

"What? Is the little girl all right? Did something else happen after I left? Is everyone OK? What's going on? Tell me. Was someone shooting guns? I thought I heard shooting. I could swear I heard gun shots, not fire crackers. Sarah did too. You know she had some bullets in her back wall. Did someone get shot?"

Dave waited until Ellie ran down.

"As I was saying, last night didn't turn out quite as well as I expected."

28

"Sorry," Ellie said. "I'm working on not interrupting. I did it again, didn't I?"

"Yep."

"It won't happen again, I promise."

"Well, I don't know if I can accept a promise that I pretty much believe won't be kept, but trying's good. Now, I'm going to continue and you can ask all you want at the end."

Ellie nodded very vigorously.

"I talked to Carrie, that's the little girl who went missing, and her parents Jean and Van, down at the station after all the hoopla quieted down last night. And that little girl told me what happened. She didn't just get lost. She got picked up by a man. Could be the same man you told me you saw, Ellie."

Dave held his hand up like he was directing traffic. "Hold on. I'm getting to it. The man picked her up from behind with one hand and covered her eyes and mouth with the other. She tried to scream and struggle, but he held her too tightly. He didn't say anything to her that she remembered except that he wasn't going to hurt her and to just keep quiet. She couldn't see anything because he kept his hand over her eyes."

"Oh no. That's awful. Poor little thing."

Dave continued with a scowl at Ellie. "She thinks he carried her only a little way, not too far, because she was crying and still wiggling trying to get away. Then, the man put her on the ground. By the time she got herself turned around, he was gone. She never saw him at all, not when he grabbed her and not after he put her down."

"Terrible, how terrible."

"Ellie, stop interrupting. After he left her, she didn't know where she was and she was too scared to call out in case the man was still near, so she just sat in the dark. She said she saw some of the fireworks going off but couldn't figure out which way to go to find her parents. After the fireworks stopped she was afraid her family would go home without her, so she got up and started walking. That's when one of the guys searching for her found her. Only a couple of hundred yards away from where she started, but out back of the clubhouse."

"Wow!"

"So, I need a good description of that man you saw. You're the only one I know of who mentioned seeing a suspicious looking man."

"Oh dear. I hope I can remember. The whole thing is just so distressing. Poor child."

"Ellie, can you describe him?"

"I really didn't look at him that long. But I know he was wearing dark clothes, a t-shirt and long pants. I think his hair was dark. Yes, it must have been or I would've noticed it reflecting the light from the fireworks like Carrie's hair did. He had dark hair. Now I'm sure about that. I don't think he was too tall. But he wasn't short either. Medium? No, not really. More tall than medium, I guess.

"I remember he was carrying a blanket and he was watching everyone. He just stood there watching the crowd and looking angry. Right! I remember. His mouth turned down at the corners like he was scowling or irritated. I remember thinking that he was the only one in Hummingbird Falls who wasn't having a good time."

Ellie stopped to think. She pictured the man standing by the cedar bushes. She concentrated and tried to focus the image, use a kind of telephoto lens approach, to make him appear closer and bigger so she could see the details more clearly. It didn't work very well.

"I'm sorry. The only other thing I can remember about him is that his face seemed so white, or pale, like he hadn't been in the sun at all. But everything was so chaotic last night, with the noise and all the people milling about. I didn't really see him all that well. But I can tell you I got shivers just looking at him."

"You did good, Ellie, to notice him at all. Your observation skills may help us nab this guy. Now, I have to tell you something else. I don't know whether it connects to this man you saw or not. And, all this information is strictly confidential. I'm only telling you because you're my only witness to this guy. You can't tell anyone, not even Sarah. Can you promise me that?"

Ellie reflected. "I think I can promise you that, Dave. Plus, I've been holding on to some other things that maybe I better tell you too, in strictest confidence, as well. I promised these people I wouldn't reveal their names. But now that this has happened to Carrie, and she's Jean's daughter, I think I better tell you everything."

"I can't believe this, Ellie. Are you keeping important things from me again? After what happened last summer? I thought you learned your lesson."

"I did, I did," Ellie pleaded. "This all just happened and I don't know if it is really important or just nonsense. I wanted to check it out a little myself before I bothered you or embarrassed myself. I know you're so busy."

"Baloney, Ellie. You know I'm never too busy to listen to police business. If you had called me, I would have made time for you."

"But I did call and you weren't there. And Sarah called."

"Did you tell the dispatcher it was important and you needed to talk to me?"

"Well, not exactly. I wasn't really calling about everything before, just about the gun shots I heard. Now, that you tell me this man I saw may be dangerous, a couple of things I've been checking out seem to fit together."

"Alright, alright. Get to it. Tell me now, Ellie. What's going on?"

Ellie proceeded to tell Dave about Jean and Alma coming into the library and confiding what they overheard in the deli. She filled Dave in on Reggie's comments and description of the couple. Then she described how she found the riddle in the Agatha Christie mystery in the library, solved it and found another riddle in the china cup by Black Bear Bridge. She explained she hadn't been able to solve the second riddle yet and that she had found a third riddle on her windshield last night. She confessed that she had worked to narrow her list of clue writing suspects to ten, using the library keys and people she remembered being in the library as starting points. She finished by describing the contents of the note left on her windshield at the fireworks and how it warned her to hurry up and solve the second riddle, that time was running out.

"That's quite a story, Ellie. Sometimes I just can't figure out what to do with you," said Dave rubbing his lower back. He added, "My back is killing me."

"Why don't you sit down. Maybe that would help."

"I don't think sitting down is going to solve the pain in the, um, back that I've got now, Ellie. But I'll try anything right about now. How 'bout another cup of coffee?"

Ellie was so relieved that Dave wasn't yelling at her for investigating mysteries without informing him or for withholding evidence that could aid him in his investigation, that she practically ran into the kitchen for the coffee. She added six cookies to his saucer and brought it in to him.

"Ellie. You laid things out for me. I'm a little skeptical about what kind of crime, if any, Jean and Alma heard about. And the riddles you found could have come from anyone for any number of reasons. After all, you do have a reputation as an amateur snoop, umm, I mean sleuth. Someone is probably just testing you out or pulling a good one that we'll hear about for months at the Pastry Shop if you're fooled."

"But Dave," Ellie protested.

"Ellie, I listened to you, now listen to me. You've told me some things in confidence that are going on with you. And my advice is to stay calm, have fun solving those riddles and see what turns up in the end. Maybe you're in for a great wonderful surprise. It could go that way, as well as the way you're worried about."

"But Dave."

"Ellie, hold on. You had your turn. Now let me finish mine please. I'm going to tell you my information as I intended to before we got into the riddle stuff. There's been a lot going on in my world, too. And it's very important police business. Maybe your incidents and mine will have some connection. If so, I'm willing to work with you on aspects of what's going on. But you have to keep me informed at all times, no matter what. And no more investigating on your own. We have a serious problem here and I don't want the official investigation contaminated in any way. Got it?"

"Absolutely, Dave, in no uncertain terms. I will keep you totally 100% up to date."

"I'll take your word for it. Now, besides the episode last night with Carrie, there was a reported attempted child abduction in Greenberg just last week. It hasn't been publicized because the Greenberg Police want to protect the victim and her family, who were not touched or hurt in any way, except of course they were very frightened."

"How awful," Ellie said, restraining herself from uttering more than two words with a failing effort. She added, "Do you think it's the same man?"

"I don't know. But the two events happening so close together give me concern. It could be the start of a new series of child abductions or it could be some child abuser, just released from prison, returning to his old patterns. Or it could be an initial attempt at kidnapping or abduction by some inexperienced, confused young man. But that's not all. Let me finish.

"There's more?"

"Ellie, sometimes you drive me nuts. Yes, there's more. I received a call from Bill Crandall of the SBI. He informed me that a dead woman was found in the White Mountain State Park, close to the boundary of Hummingbird Falls. She was murdered. Shot with buck shot. They found her body at the Crooked River, across from the Crooked Heart."

"Crooked Heart? Did you say Crooked Heart?"

"Yes, why?"

"What's the Crooked Heart?"

"It's an island, formed where the Crooked River splits in two. They call it the Crooked Heart because it's shaped somewhat like a heart. Why?"

"That's what the riddle told me to do. Find the Crooked Heart where the river splits. Oh no, that means that the riddler must know about the dead woman. He must be the murderer because no one other than the police knew about the dead woman. And, of course, the killer. And he's after me, probably because of what Jean and Alma told me, and after Sarah because she's my friend, and who knows who else he's gunning for. Oh my goodness. Maybe the murderer is the one who took Carrie to threaten Jean and Alma to keep their mouths shut about what they heard. What are we going to do?"

"Hold on, Ellie, hold on."

"Oh no, that's horrible, unbelievable," Ellie gasped paying no attention to Dave. She wanted to run and hide, grab Buddy and head for the car and get out of town. She didn't know what to do. She was totally overwhelmed.

Dave tried to calm her down. "Ellie, just breathe and try to relax. You're getting ahead of yourself. Here take a drink of my coffee."

Ellie took a gulp of coffee and started to choke. "It doesn't have any milk or sugar in it. It's awful. How can you drink it this way?" She sputtered as she got her coughing under control.

"That's better. At least you still have some sense of humor left. You'll be okay."

"I won't be okay. Oh no. Not until we catch that maniac out there. Oh no. If he took little Carrie to warn Jean and Alma from telling they heard him planning to murder a woman, then he really is one horrible heartless man. And, it means he's trying to cover up that he killed the woman found at the Park. And then he's sending these notes to me so I'll go to the Crooked Heart where he can kill me too before I tell you about what Jean and Alma heard. And he's shooting at Sarah because he knows she's my friend and would probably be in on solving the riddles with me and so he wants to kill her too. Maybe he's even shooting all over town and the woods, so it will look like hunters shot the woman by accident. It all seems to fit. Oh Dave. Jean and Alma and all their kids and me and Sarah. And the poor dead woman. We're all going to be killed. This is terrible. What are you going to do, Dave?"

Dave stood up. He towered over Ellie. "Stop right now, Ellie. Get a grip. You're constructing a house of cards here. Pull any one and the whole pile falls. Everything you just pointed out is circumstantial, coincidental, hypotheses, and just plain speculation. Take a minute and let your analytical mind conquer your impulsive side for a moment. Please."

Dave paused. Ellie breathed. Buddy looked at them both. Dave sat back down.

Ellie said, "Okay. I'm calming down. I'm regathered so to speak."

"Okay. Then let's go on. I'm going to finish telling you the facts as we know them now. Is that all right with you?"

Ellie nodded yes.

Dave proceeded to lay down the rules again about Ellie keeping all that she hears to herself and that she is to do nothing without consulting him first, and that means letting him know about any gun shots she hears, any notes she receives, and any information she garners from anybody.

Ellie was bursting with the need to know everything and right away. She wanted to ask questions in the order of her own priorities and to get answers that would help her situation, but she knew better than to try that with Dave. He'd tell her in his way, in his time, not hers. So, Ellie bit her tongue again and let Dave continue.

"Hey, you're doing good, Ellie. You must have been practicing. You haven't interrupted me for at least five minutes."

"I'm trying really hard, believe me, Dave," Ellie said with a grimace. "Please go on."

"The ME found nine buck shot in her back. Two of them ripped through her back and entered the dead woman's heart. That's what killed her."

Ellie burst out again. "Dave, those are the same kind of bullets that Officer O'Rourke pulled out of Sarah's back wall, aren't they? Oh my goodness. The murderer's definitely trying to kill Sarah too!"

"Don't go so fast, Ellie. I'm checking that out right now. I sent the buck shot from Sarah's wall up to SBI to test out, just in case. But, I don't see how Sarah could have any connection with the murdered woman."

"But Sarah knows me, who knows Jean and Alma, who saw the couple in the deli, who were planning on getting rid of a woman. Who is she? I mean, who was she, the murdered woman?"

"Well, actually we don't know. She hasn't been identified yet."

"Then you don't know whether there's any connection to Sarah or not. We do know Sarah is my friend. That's probably enough for that crazy killer. We have to warn Sarah, give her protective custody, and put her in an inn where the killer won't find her."

"Slow down, Ellie. Don't make me sorry I told you about this. One step at a time. I've hired a new officer for the summer. Her name is Rosie O'Rourke. I guess you already heard about her from Sarah. She has great credentials although this is her first job right out of the academy. I'm going to assign her to patrol around Sarah's neighborhood and have her stop in the Post Office regularly. With an extra officer we'll be able to cover more bases."

"Are you going to tell Sarah?"

"Not yet. If the buck shot match up, then of course we'll alert her, even though we still may be looking at pure coincidence. It's near to impossible to match individual shot, especially when there are no casings to compare, but they're going to try. But until they get a match, then, no. And you aren't going to tell her either, Ellie."

"No, of course not, Dave. Mum's the word until you give me the okay."

"Right. Good. Now here's how you can help me now. Do you think you can identify that man at the fire works from a picture? I'm drawing up a list of all known pedophiles, registered sex offenders, suspicious males from around this area. We have a mug book of pictures of most of them, especially those who have been arrested and booked for any kind of felony. I want you to look through those pictures this morning."

"You have books of these guys? There's that many? I can't believe there would be so many bad guys around here."

"Actually, none of them lives in Hummingbird Falls. They're in the county, down in lower section of the state for the most part. Will you try to find him in the books for us?"

"Sure. I'll come down right now. Do you think the man at the fireworks could be the same man who killed the woman in the Park?"

"Right now, there isn't any reason to connect the two, other than your premise that the man took Carrie to warn Jean and Alma. Sorry, but that seems pretty far fetched to me. So, we're focusing more on child molesters, sexual deviants, and that sort. But every known felon in this area is in the books, no matter what they did, not just pedophiles."

"So, I'll be looking at a bunch of very bad guys?"

"Yep. We're working with the Greenberg Police on this case and we'll be putting out a press bulletin soon asking anyone with any information to come forward, to report any suspicious men. I know our phones will be ringing round the clock with callers. Everyone knows someone who looks suspicious. Hopefully, we'll pick up a tip that will lead to this perp. But we're not releasing any information about the Mount Washington Park Homicide or about the dead woman yet. Bill Crandall's handling that case and he wants to wait until they've checked out the forensics first. So not a word about that, right? And no mention of the Crooked Heart."

Ellie turned off the coffee pot, put on her shoes and grabbed her purse, car keys and Buddy's leash. "Right and ready."

She would have to call Mike and Sarah later. It will be so hard not to tell them what was really going on. But, she had to do what Dave told her and the police business Dave had assigned her was top priority. After that, she'd ask Dave to look at the riddles themselves. Hopefully he would authenticate the seriousness of notes and start an investigation. She didn't really understand why he paid so little attention to them. She'd have to find a way to convey the seriousness of the warnings. Then, Sarah and she would work to solve the mystery of the shots in the woods and try to find if they had any connection to everything else that was going on.

29

Ellie followed Dave all the way down to the Hummingbird Falls Police Station which was located in the basement of the Town Hall. Dave put Ellie in his office chair and brought in several loose leafed books and dropped them down in front of her.

"Go for it, Ellie. If you see anyone who looks the least bit like the man you saw last night, mark the page. I don't care if you're not sure. If he catches your attention, mark the page. I'll leave you to it. I've got a lot of calls to make."

Dave closed the office door and Ellie tentatively opened the first book. Row after row of black and white photos of unhappy looking men stared out at her. She wondered what they had done to earn a picture in this horrid book. But she put those thoughts away and focused on the job before her. She was looking for a bad man who probably was the one who had almost ruined the Fourth of July holiday and the lives of a lot of people last night. She wanted his picture to jump out at her so she could name him and rest easy that his threat to good people's happiness was eliminated for good.

It seemed like hours had gone by. Bonnie, the pretty town hall secretary and Ellie's friend came downstairs with a blueberry turnover from the Pastry Shop and peaked in the door.

"Want a break Ellie? I've got turnovers."

Ellie smiled and put a marker in the book she was examining. "I'd love a break and especially, a turnover. Thanks Bonnie."

"I heard you were down here. I thought you might want to hear some new gossip."

"Always," Ellie mumbled with her mouth full. Ellie could tell Bonnie wanted to know what Ellie was doing, but Ellie managed to keep her mouth shut just like Dave had warned her to. She kept in mind that he wasn't releasing any information until the press conference called for this afternoon. And what she was doing would reach the Pastry Shop before the papers if she told Bonnie.

"Those people who rented your old cottage are outsiders, from somewhere in New York," Bonnie said.

"How do you know?" asked Ellie, her mouth still stuffed full of blueberry turnover.

"They came to the Town offices to complain the other day. They're very strange. Their names are Todd and Millie Buckley and they have three kids. They came in to find out about trash pickup and were really upset that they had to take their own trash to the dump and that we had no pick up services. Where do they think they are?"

"Anything else weird about them? Lots of people don't know about dumps anymore. In some towns you aren't even allowed to enter the dump. They call them land fills, now. Only official trash collectors are allowed to use the dump site and they have to pay a huge fee. And homeowners have to buy certified trash containers from the city. They aren't even allowed to use their own containers."

"Is that so? Can you believe that? That's just awful. I love going to the dump. I wouldn't miss it for anything. I meet all my friends and neighbors there and I usually find wonderful treasures that others throw away. It's free and it's fun. I'm glad the city ways haven't reached Hummingbird Falls."

"Me, too. Tell me more about the Buckleys."

"I really don't know how to describe them. Oh yeah. They come from New York. They just don't look like they'll fit in here very well. They dress up like they're going to a party, all fancy and such. They didn't want to put the dump sticker on their windshield. Said it looked tacky. And they were complaining because we don't have a bank, video store or a supermarket in town. I tried to explain that we like it that way, but they looked at me like I was crazy or something."

"Sounds like they're not accustomed to country life. Maybe when I'm finished here, I'll ride by and stop to say hello and check them out, Bonnie. I'll let you know what I think. Do you know anything more about them?"

"I'm working on it, Ellie. There's a lot of buzz about them at the Pastry Shop. Seems like the oldest kid wears diamond ear rings and some one said he's probably in a gang. New York has a lot of gangs, I guess."

"Anything else?"

"Well, I didn't want to say anything to you about it, but I guess you will find out soon enough. Mike says the cottage is a mess. Looks like they're trashing the place."

"What? My old cottage? That sweet lovely, cozy cottage? How could they do that? That's terrible."

"Ellie, that's what Mike said and you know how persnickety he is. Don't jump to conclusions until you see for yourself. That's what I always remind myself after I've heard the gossip in the Pastry Shop."

"Well, after I'm finished here, I'm definitely going to check the cottage out. Thanks for telling me. I'll drive right up there, you can be sure of that. What I'll do if it's true, I don't know. But I'll tell you this, I won't allow anyone to trash that cottage. You can count on that.

" Right now, though, I have to get back on task. And no, I can't tell you what I'm doing. Strictly confidential, according to Dave. So my mouth's buttoned."

Bonnie looked disappointed, but she knew Dave's instructions were fixed like concrete, so she just waved good bye and went back upstairs.

Ellie returned to her job, studying each picture carefully and turning page after page with no results. Every now and again Dave brought her a refill of coffee. Every so often she took a break and walked Buddy outside for a few minutes.

Ellie finished book after book in her search for the strange man she saw last night at the firework display. She was on the last book when a face suddenly caught her attention. The cranky looking man had a decided turned down mouth and deep jowls. He could be the one she saw. Ellie marked the page and continued on until finally she had viewed every picture. Only one man out of all the hundreds she'd looked at seemed familiar. She turned back to the page she'd marked. Yes, that looked like the man she saw.

Ellie left the office to find Dave. She saw him on the phone in another office and waved to him. He mouthed, "Wait. I'll be right with you."

Ellie walked around outside stretching her legs and letting Buddy take a little run. As she was heading back inside, Colby drove in and came up to the door. His handsome looks, buff physique, and easy smile were hard to resist. His reputation as a ladies' man was enhanced by his charming way of looking directly into a woman's eyes with his long black lashes blinking over his sky blue eyes. He appeared shy and bashful while remaining completely masculine and capable.

"Find any one, Ellie?" Colby smiled.

"One guy looked right to me. But when I noticed him last night dusk was just turning into dark and I didn't see him very long. He seemed to disappear just after I first saw him so I'm afraid I can't really be positive. If he were in front of me, I think I could match his looks with his shape and be more certain."

"Hopefully, that can happen. We'll check out who you identified and bring him in. Then you can get a better look."

"Will he know it's me?"

"No. We have a one way mirror in the interrogation room, Ellie. You can see in, but he can't see you. And of course, we'll never tell him who the witness is. So you're safe."

"Good. Even thinking about that man gives me the creeps."

"Let's go in and see who you picked," Colby said as he held the door for Ellie. They walked back into the office she was using. Ellie showed him the picture.

"Hmmm. Let me get this number and check it out on the computer."

Colby sat down at Dave's desk and turned on the computer. He waited for a few minutes while the older machine booted up and then typed slowly with one finger. The screen flickered and flashed and Colby clicked a few more keys and waited.

"Gotcha," he muttered. The printer whirled and then slowly spit a paper out. Colby picked it up and read it quickly. He slapped the paper down on the desk in front of Ellie.

Ellie looked up at Colby. "Is this him?"

"Ellie, you picked a real mean guy. His name is George Bamdina. He's a member of a New York mob. He has a long record of arrests and indictments. He's been in prison for several felonies including second degree murder. He's only been out for a few weeks."

"Oh my. Then he really is a bad guy," Ellie gasped.

"Oh yeah, he's bad all right. I wonder what he's doing in Hummingbird Falls. He isn't known as a pedophile, so I don't think he's the one who picked up Carrie. But who knows? These bad guys can fool you."

"Well, what now?"

"I'll give this i.d. to Dave and see what he says. I'll be right back."

Colby left the room. Ellie had found the man she saw last night and he turned out to be a real criminal. Maybe now he was going to be arrested and sent back to jail. Just like that. It had all happened so fast. She didn't quite know how to feel. Glad to have this awful episode over and mad that someone could just get out of jail and then go back to a life of breaking the law and hurting people. Maybe these guys shouldn't be let out of jail ever.

Dave came in with Colby. "Thanks, Ellie. We've called Greenberg and let them know that Bamdina is known to be in the area. They'll be keeping a look out for him, too. Bill Crandall of the SBI has been notified as well. So, we have an all points bulletin out for him. We'll find him if he's still around. But knowing his kind, if he has finished his business he'll be long gone. If he still has his work to do, then he's here somewhere waiting for his chance to get it done."

"What's his business? It can't be scaring little girls."

"Nope. He's never been mixed up with that. His specialty is contract work. Killing for money."

"You mean someone has paid him to kill someone in Hummingbird Falls?"

"We don't know that, Ellie. Don't go there. All we know is that a known mob killer has been spotted in our village. Put that together with a dead woman in the State Park, shots going off at all hours, a little girl who was scared by someone last night? I don't know what to tell you. Maybe George Bamdina is only here to see the fireworks and the famous Falls."

Colby laughed. "Sure, boss, sure. That guy doesn't do anything without a reason. He's here for something. I bet he killed that woman."

"Just take it one step at a time, Colby. Don't go getting tunnel vision. You miss things when you lose your objectivity. As far as we know everyone's a suspect in that killing and in that attempted abduction until we have a confession or a witness who actually saw what happened. Keep your eyes open. Get Officer O'Rourke up to date and make sure she knows the procedure to follow in case she spots him. Bill Crandall will get back to us with more details about Bamdina's car, license, etc. Till then, just keep cool."

"How's Officer O'Rourke doing so far?" Ellie asked.

"Well, she's doing fine. We've been busier than usual and she happened to be recommended and available and seems up to the job. So we're trying her out."

"She must be the one I saw last night, directing traffic. It sure was fun to watch her. She gathered quite a crowd."

Colby grunted, "Fun to watch, pretty, with a knock out figure. Not my kind of cop. Probably be a great date, but I don't trust her as back up if we get into a tight situation."

Dave interrupted. "Why? Because she's a woman? Grow up, Colby. Women are more than just potential dates. Rosie graduated at the top of her class at the academy. If you don't trust her, then meet her out at the shooting range and see if you can beat her at the targets. I did. I tried. I lost. She can shoot. She's smart. And right now, I'm happy to have her around."

"Yes sir," Colby answered.

Dave turned to Ellie. "We owe you our thanks, Ellie, for spotting this guy and for picking him out. Now, why don't you go home and relax? You've been here for hours. If we need you again, we'll give you a call."

"Will you call me when you catch him and he's in jail again? I'd just feel better knowing he was under lock and key."

"Sure, Ellie. No problem. I'll give you a call just as soon as I hear. And don't worry. It may be that you won't have to identify him in court. After all, we don't know that he's guilty of anything yet. Or if we pick him up maybe he'll just confess the whole thing. Some of these guys want to go back to jail. They feel more at home there. I know it sounds odd, but often they'll violate parole on purpose to get sent back. That makes it easy for us because then they don't need any urging to tell us exactly what they did."

Ellie gathered her things and hooked Buddy up to his leash, pondering why someone would want to make jail his home. "It takes all kinds, they say," a cliché the only answer she could come up with.

"Talk with you later, guys. Dave, I hope you'll follow up with me about those riddles as soon as you can. I still think they're important and have something to do with what's going on. And by the way, I'm awfully glad you two are right here keeping us all safe and Officer O'Rourke as well."

Buddy and Ellie drove home. On the way, she stopped by the cottage where she'd spent ten wonderful summers. No car was in the driveway, but she got out and walked up to the front porch anyway. The porch was crowded with empty cardboard boxes and black plastic trash bags and smelled like rotten garbage. Most of the bags were ripped apart and moldy, spoiled food was scattered all over the porch, steps and front yard. Some broken plastic lawn chairs were thrown in one corner. She sighed. Her lovely porch and yard. Such a mess.

Ellie knocked on the door. She waited and knocked again but there were no sounds from inside. She turned and walked down the steps trying not to look at the dried up perennials that she'd babied and cared for over the years. She shook her head.

She just didn't understand some people and never would. How could someone let a plant die from lack of water? What kind of person would throw trash on their front porch? As Ellie made her way to the car, she reminded herself not to judge. Maybe their move had been traumatic. Maybe their lives have been troubled and they were starting again and were slow to learn new ways, and care for themselves and what was around them.

Ellie practiced the Zen of compassion and pushed the ugly negative thoughts out of her mind. But she'd stop by again and soon. And she'd offer to help the Buckley's with their trash situation. She would even ask them if they wanted help with the gardens. Maybe a little friendly encouragement would help to change their ways. If the situation didn't improve and soon, then she would have to take matters into her own hands. She wasn't quite sure what she would do, but she'd do something.

Most of the day had passed and late afternoon shadows covered the road as Ellie and Buddy drove back up the long driveway and parked outside their beautiful cabin. Ellie poured a tall glass of ice tea, gave Buddy some ice water and settled down in her favorite rocker on the back screen porch and reflected on the last couple of weeks. Was it only two weeks ago that her grandson had been bundled up in his car seat and with her son and daughter-in-law drove away? Ellie thought of little Carrie and her trauma of last night. Ellie knew her own children would guard her grandson vigilantly, but she worried about all the other kids in the world. Who was watching out for them? When would women and children be safe in this world?

30

Ellie, sleeping soundly, had forgotten all about the mystery of the gun shots until something woke her up in the middle of the night. Buddy started barking and jumped off the bed and ran out of the room toward the back porch. The motion lights popped on leaking some light indoors. Leaving the inside lights off so she wouldn't become a target, she ran after Buddy, afraid he might get hurt.

Ellie peered out the window into the dark. The moon had grown to a small sliver in the eastern sky, but gave so little light that she can see nothing but dark shadows on darker background outside the bright glare of the motion lights. But as she continued to stare outside and her eyes accustomed to the shades of black, she saw a dark form move low against the darker background. Someone was out there behind her house, moving in the deeper dark of the woods.

Ellie dialed 911. Buddy was barking so loudly that she can hardly hear the dispatcher say, "What's your emergency?"

"There's someone outside my house, sneaking around."

"Who is this please and what is your address?"

"Ellie Hastings, Foster Brook Road, the new cabin up on Foster Brook."

"Yes, Ms. Hastings. Tell me what's happening."

"I woke up. My dog started to growl. Then my motion lights went on and my dog went crazy. I think I saw someone in the woods."

"Are you all right?"

"No, I'm not all right. I'm scared to death. Send someone to help me. I'm all alone here, except for my dog."

"Secure your doors and windows and keep calm. An officer has been notified and will be there shortly."

"Who am I talking to?"

"Ms. Hastings, I'm Betsy Wilson. I've seen you at the Little Church on Sundays. Chief Shaffer and Colby Conners are over at Greenberg tonight assisting at the Fourth of July celebration, but Officer O'Rourke is deputized and on call tonight. I've notified her and she will be there very shortly. I'm sure everything will be just fine."

"But I don't know who's out there. He could be watching me right this minute and waiting for the lights to go off. Oh my gosh, they just went off."

"Take it easy, Ms. Hastings. Most motion lighting works on a timer. After a few moments of no motion, they turn off. You must have an indoor switch that can turn them on manually, by passing the timer."

"Yes, I do. Hold on while I go to the switch."

"I'll be right here with you unless I have another call."

Ellie ran to the bank of switches by the kitchen door. The top one controlled the outside lights. She clicked it on and the outdoor lights glared whitely against the dark once again. She ran back to the phone.

"Oh, thank you. I have the lights on again."

"Good, I'm sorry Ms. Hastings, but I have another call, in fact two. I'll have to put you on hold. Please keep your line open until Officer O'Rourke gets there. I have to leave you now. Don't worry. The officer should be there any minute. You'll be fine."

"Thanks," Ellie said and listened to the silence on the other end of the phone. She didn't want to put the phone down. It was the only thing connecting her to help. She stood there feeling awfully alone. Buddy stopped running back and forth and walked over and rubbed up against her knee.

"At least you stopped barking, Buddy. Does that mean we're OK? Has the bad person left?"

Buddy just looked at her. His head tipped as if considering the question. Ellie moved closer toward the front door to watch for Officer O'Rourke. She felt like her cabin was enclosed in a wall of bright light, barely keeping the darkness from clutching Buddy and her in its grip. She hoped Officer O'Rourke would hurry.

Minutes passed by. No sign of a car racing down her driveway. Her eyes moved constantly between the driveway and her watch. Ten, then fifteen minutes passed. Where was Officer O'Rourke?

Ellie yelled into the silent phone. "Help. Come back on line Betsy. Where are you?"

Then she realized that she needed to hang up and call 911 again. She did and received a busy signal. She redialed. Another busy signal.

Then Ellie heard the slap of the back screen porch door. Buddy ran from her side barking wildly, heading for the door to the porch. Darn it. She'd been focusing for fifteen minutes on the front driveway waiting for the police and hadn't been watching out back. Someone was out there now, on her porch.

Ellie huddled down low to the floor and crawled on her hands and knees to hide behind the living room couch.

She whispered, "Buddy, come here. Buddy, shhhhh. Come here."

But Buddy was too worked up to hear her. He continued to bark and growl at the door leading to the back screen porch. At least his fierce barking might keep the intruder at bay and make him think twice about breaking in. But what if he was the one who had been shooting all over with a gun? Would he just shoot Buddy to get him out of the way? And what did he want? Why was he here? Why me? Ellie's mind was in a whirl.

Vicious scary thoughts of bludgeoning, rape, and murder ran through her mind. She pictured the dead woman in the Crooked River and a body in the library. She'd been in tight spots before, but never before had she been so terrified in her own home, her own sanctuary. Not since the bear episode that was.

That thought did it. She started to get mad. A woman's home was her castle and Ellie'd be darned if someone was going to terrorize her in her beloved home. She got to her knees and crawled over to the window that looked over the back porch. Fueled by her adrenalin she pulled herself up and peeked under the curtain and looked out on the back porch.

31

She didn't believe what she saw. Climbing over the rattan love seat, clutching at her porch rocker, careening from the floor lamp shade, capering across the flag stone floor were a huge mother raccoon and three of the cutest baby raccoons she'd ever seen. Ellie stood up and pulled the curtain aside and stared at the mayhem metamorphisizing on the porch. The raccoons chewed the cushions and threw them to the floor. They tipped the waste baskets over, emptied them and pawed through every piece of debris. They nibbled plants, dug the potting soil out and pushed it across the floor. They tried to wash their paws in Ellie's indoor water feature, a small waterfall dripping into a shallow base before being pumped back up to complete the circuit. Then they played in the water and rolled in the dirt, making a muddy mess of everything. Before her very eyes, her beautiful screen porch, her sacred place of calm peace and tranquility was turning into a quagmire of horror.

Just then she heard a siren screaming down her driveway. She ran to the front door, unlocked it and hurried down the front steps to meet Officer O'Rourke.

Seeing Ellie's wild rush, Officer O'Rourke pulled her rifle out of the gun rack and yelled, "Where is he? You get in my truck now and lock the doors. Radio to Betsy and tell her to send reinforcements. Where is he?"

Out of breath, Ellie leaned over to suck in air and as she sucked it in she started to laugh. She rose out of her crouch and roaring with laughter tried to communicate with Officer O'Rourke about what happened. She didn't get two words out before she collapsed in hysterical whooping again.

Officer O'Rourke didn't know what to do. She looked around, searching for danger while she quizzed Ellie.

"Talk to me. Did he hurt you, Ms. Hastings? Calm down. Tell me what's going on. Stop it. You're hysterical. Talk to me."

Ellie just couldn't help it. All her fear turned to giddy giggles. Finally, she calmed down enough to gasp out, "raccoons, four raccoons, back porch."

Officer O'Rourke lowered her gun. "Ms. Hastings, are you telling me all this is about raccoons? You better stop laughing and tell me what's going on."

She was serious. She was glaring at Ellie in such a very serious way that Ellie shut right up. Ellie started to tell her the whole story right from the beginning, but Officer O'Rourke interrupted her.

"Now Ms. Hastings, don't go on and on. Just tell me. Is there someone I need to worry about?"

"No, just raccoons."

Officer O'Rourke lowered her gun further. "Good God, you had me scared out of my mind. Why'd you call 911 and get Betsy all worked up?"

Ellie started to tell the story once more and again Officer O'Rourke interrupted her before she got very far.

"No, Ms. Hastings, I don't want the whole story bit by bit. Just tell me if there's any danger right now."

Ellie shook her head no. "Just raccoons destroying my porch. By the way you can call me Ellie. Everyone does."

"Thank you, Ellie. I'm Rosie O'Rourke. I'm a summer hire, just started July 3, to help out with the festivities. Sorry it took me a while to get here. I'm not familiar with all the back roads. Now, please show me what you're talking about."

They walked around to the back of the house. The outside lights made the porch stage bright and through the screen they saw the four raccoons romping and chirring and playing. The raccoons didn't pay any attention to the two women watching them.

Rosie just stood there staring and shaking her head.

"Now, Ellie. I'm going to call Betsy and let her know what's happening here and then I'm coming back, opening that screen door all the way so the raccoons have an exit route and then I'm going to hear your whole story. I want you to go in and make me a good strong cup of coffee if you don't mind. Can you do that?"

Ellie nodded yes and walked with Officer Rosie back to the front of the house. While Rosie called Betsy on the car radio, Ellie went into the house, calmed Buddy down and made a pot of coffee. She was beginning to feel a little foolish again.

In a few minutes Rosie came into the kitchen and sat down at the table. She looked up at Ellie and said, "OK. Now go to it, Ellie. You have until I drink this cup of coffee to fill me in on exactly what happened here and then I have another call I have to check out. Make it good or I might just have to arrest you for disturbing the law."

She smiled at Ellie while she emptied three spoonfuls of sugar into her coffee cup and then took a gulp of the steaming brew. Ellie approved of her right away.

Ellie talked Rosie's ear off for the next five minutes, while Rosie finished her coffee and ate four cookies. Then Rosie walked to back of the cabin, opened the porch screen door as far as it would go and secured it with a rock. She walked back around and entered the front door, moved to the inside screen porch door, opened it and yelled at the raccoons while she clapped her hands loudly. Raccoons scampered all over looking for an escape and finally in excited scurries exited out the screen door and bolted for the woods. Rosie closed and locked the screen door. Ellie kept talking about what happened all the way out to the big black Hummingbird Falls Police SUV that Rosie was driving. Ellie was still talking when Rosie started the truck up.

"Gotta go, Ellie. Keep the lights on tonight. Those raccoons might come back, might not. But they're only raccoons. Leave Buddy on the porch for a little while each night and they'll stop coming."

Ellie nodded and asked, "Where are you going now?"

"Got a call about gun shots about three or four miles down the road toward town. Marshall's farm. I'm going to check in with them and see what they heard."

"What's all the shooting about, Rosie?"

"Don't know whether it's shooting or not, Ellie. Just reports about sounds that sound like shooting going on all yesterday and today, which just happens to be the third and fourth of July. Now everyone knows that anyone who smuggled fireworks over the state line will be setting them off right and left. But people still insist on calling saying they heard gun shots. Maybe they did. Maybe there were both fireworks and gun shots."

"Well, I'll have you know, I called myself yesterday. Sure sounded like a gun. What if it's shooting and not fire crackers?"

"Just one thing at a time, Ellie. One thing at a time. I'm just checking it out. If someone's shooting firecrackers or guns we'll find out about it, don't you worry. Meanwhile, if anything else scares you up here, call Betsy."

"Thanks, Rosie. I really was scared tonight when I heard all that noise on the porch, but I'm sorry I bothered you about something that just turned out to be nature mixing it up with civilization. I'll check things out more carefully before I call again. I promise."

"Glad to help you out, Ellie. Nice to meet you. Stay safe. See you later."

Little did either of them know that they would see each other later, but under much less pleasant circumstances.

32

The next morning Ellie decided she and Buddy would visit the Pastry Shop to get her blueberry turnover fix and find out what people thought about what was going on in Hummingbird Falls.

When she opened the door, the buzz of voices was droning loud. The place was filled. Without exception, everyone in the place looked up to see who was coming in. Even those with their backs to the door turned to observe the new comer. When they saw it was Ellie, several waved hands or nodded heads and others shouted, "Hi, Ellie."

Ellie waved and turned to give Elizabeth her order. "I'm going wild today, Elizabeth. I'm going to have a chocolate croissant with my coffee."

Elizabeth looked startled. "What's up, Ellie? You only order chocolate scones or croissants when you're up to something. It's a dead giveaway. Do you know something about what's going on?"

Ellie tried to look innocent, a stretch for her. "What's going on?" she asked Elizabeth in her sweetest voice.

"You know. Lots of stuff. What happened to Sarah's house, the gun shots all over town. Those new people. And other things I can't really talk about. Take your choice."

Ellie was relieved that the murder in the State Park and the true story of what happened to Carrie was not mentioned. Dave must have managed to keep that quiet so far. She was so pleased about that she failed to notice the comment Elizabeth made about "other things."

"Elizabeth, I'm so busy with the library, my reading and writing, and my new gardens, I hardly have time to think, let alone get involved with the mysteries in this village."

Elizabeth laughed. "That's a good one, Ellie. If I didn't know better, I might even believe you."

Ellie picked up her coffee and croissant and walked over to the table where Sarah, Bonnie, and Margaret were sitting. She sat down and settled Buddy next to the booth, but out of the way of human feet.

"Ellie, hi. Sorry, but we all have to leave in just a minute. Our breaks are over," said Sarah, exchanging glances with the other women. "So we have to talk fast."

"That's okay. Hi to you all and how are you? I'm sorry I missed you at the fireworks. Weren't they grand?"

"Absolutely stupendous," Sarah answered. "And how are you? Bonnie told us you were over at the Police Station for hours yesterday. Are you in trouble? What's going on?"

"Sorry," Bonnie said. "It just slipped out when we were talking about the Buckley's."

"What about the Buckley's?" Ellie said, trying to change the direction of the conversation.

"Oh no, you don't," said Sarah. "You first. What were you doing at the Police Station? Was it about the guns shooting at all hours?"

"No. Not really. Look, I really can't talk about it. Dave told me in no uncertain terms that it was highly confidential."

"OOOHHHHH!" the three women crowed together. "We knew it. You're into something interesting, aren't you?" asked Margaret. "If you can't talk about it, it must be really exciting. Tell us. Come on. You can trust us."

Ellie laughed. "I've already said more than I should have. Now, please. Let it be. You'll know about it soon enough. I promise you."

"Know about what, Ellie?" Margaret tried again. "I always tell you everything that I hear in the gallery. Even the most juicy items. You owe me."

"Not this time, Margaret. You will just have to accept my word. Now what's this about the Buckley's?"

"They got jobs at the Hawks Inn," said Bonnie. "Todd Buckley is taking over the bar and Millie Buckley's been hired as the hostess. Jerry, he's the new manager, was in getting his permits checked and says that he even hired their oldest kid, Matt, for kitchen work, washing dishes, salad prep and busing tables."

"My guess is they're here to stay. They're not here to just hang around living the good life of a tourist," added Margaret.

"Looks that way," said Bonnie. "Did you ride by the cottage yesterday and meet them, Ellie?"

"I stopped up there but no one was home. The cottage looked terrible. Garbage was all over the porch and the gardens looked dead. Broke my heart."

"Cheer up," Bonnie said. "Jerry told me that Todd borrowed the Inn's pickup to take a load of trash to the dump. I guess they only have a small Mustang and with the accumulation of packing boxes and other stuff they couldn't fit it all into their car, so it was piling up."

"Thank goodness for that. I'll drive by again and check it out. I want to meet them anyway. I need to wipe that bad first impression out of my mind. Maybe they'll be a nice addition to our town."

Sarah said, "I haven't seen them in the Post Office. I wonder what they're doing about their mail. I suppose they think it gets delivered to a mail slot in the front door like in the city."

The women laughed, knowing that their small village ways were the butt of many jokes as well. It felt refreshing to ridicule the city folks once in a while, although they realized the tourists' money fed the town coffers and made jobs available for many of the locals. Sarah, Margaret and Bonnie took last sips of their coffee and slid out of the booth.

"Bye Ellie. See you later."

"Bye ladies. Sarah, have you got just a minute more? I want to ask you something."

"Only a minute. I'm late already. Can't keep the Post Office shut down beyond government regulations."

"I just want to set up a time to meet with you about all that's going on. You know, what we talked about on the phone, plus something else that's come up."

"Oh, something new?" Sarah's eyes twinkled with curiosity. "I certainly can make time. How about 5:30 tonight?"

"Sounds good. Can we meet at your house?"

"Sure. I even have some good leftovers I can warm up. You like chicken pie, don't you?"

"Love it, especially your chicken pie, Sarah, with all the gravy thick with white meat and carrots, peas, and little bits of pimento. It's delicious."

"I'll see you at 5:30 then. I can't wait to hear what you've come up with. Now I really have to run. I'm late."

Sarah flew out the door. No sooner had she disappeared than James Foster walked over.

"Hey Ellie. Hello there Buddy. Just wanted to say hello. Can I sit for a minute?" James bent down and patted Buddy on the head. Buddy rewarded him with a wet lick.

Ellie looked into James soft gray eyes and felt a little warmth creeping up her cheeks. "Sure, sit down. Good to see you."

"I haven't talked with you for what seems an awfully long while. I know you've been busy with your family and we've had the holiday crazies down at the home. But now that things are quieting down, I wondered if you could have dinner with me tomorrow night?"

Ellie found her mouth had gone dry. She took a sip of her coffee. "Why that sounds really nice, James. What time and where?"

"Why don't I pick you up at 6:00 and take you to one of the Inns?"

"That sounds great, thanks. Have you got a new case you want to consult on?"

"No. I just miss you, Ellie. I want to have a quiet dinner with you. Can't talk in here. Too many eavesdroppers and rumor mongers."

Ellie laughed. "Tell me about it. I'm sure that someone right now is forming a good one about why you sat down with me."

"I don't think I would mind that kind of rumor, would you Ellie?" James asked, smiling at Ellie's blush coloring her cheeks.

"Depends, James. And that's all I care to say about that. Even the tables have ears in here. I'm looking forward to dinner though. Thanks for asking me."

"Totally my pleasure," said James rising up from the booth. "And now I have to get back to work. See you tomorrow night," he whispered with a wink. "Wait 'til they hear about that."

Ellie smiled a little self consciously. She looked around to see who was watching. Mike waved at her.

"Hey, neighbor. Stop over here on your way out. I want to talk to you about something."

Ellie finished the last of her croissant and coffee, left a small tip for Elizabeth and walked over to Mike's booth. He stood up, too.

"I'm finished here. I'll walk you out."

Ellie and Mike nodded goodbye to several people lingering over their coffee and pastries and walked out the door and into the parking lot.

"Going over to the library?"

"Yes, holiday's over. Back to work, even for me. Although I can hardly call it work. I get paid to be somewhere filled with books that I love and meet people who are wonderful. I'm a lucky woman."

"Yep, I think you are, Ellie. I've always thought so. You know that."

Ellie looked up at Mike. They had been good friends for ten years. There had been some sparks between them now and again, but nothing but a fine friendship had ever evolved.

"What do you want to talk to me about?"

119

"I've been hearing what I think are gun shots going off practically every night. I wonder if you heard them too?"

"I was going to call you and ask you that very thing, Mike. Sarah called me and wanted to know if we heard shots up on the mountain like she was hearing in town. I guess a lot of people are hearing them."

"Yep. Marshall's called the police the other night. Everyone says it sounds like a gun, maybe a shot gun, but Dave and Colby seem to think it's just firecrackers or fireworks kids have got hold of."

"Well Mike, I agree with Sarah. She thinks something funny is going on. Has anyone found any dead animals? Could it be poachers? Are there any fire arms groups that are having a shooting meet, with targets in the woods, even though that's illegal? What about those paint gun groups? I've heard they sneak onto private property to play their games."

"Don't know. I thought maybe since you had been down to the Police Station yesterday that maybe you had learned something and had the inside scoop. You remember a couple of years back when livestock started turning up killed and butchered in the fields by that black market meat syndicate? I'm wondering if I need to hire someone to ride herd on my cattle. I don't want to lose any of my herd to cattle thieves."

Ellie ignored the reference to her visit to the Police Station. It seemed everyone knew she had been there. Small towns seldom had any secrets about the everyday activity of their residents and Hummingbird Falls was no different. But secrets about personal matters and family skeletons in farmhouse closets went deep and were rarely questioned or mentioned by the locals, unless some unexpected incident occurred that brought the secret to light.

"I haven't thought about that. Has anyone lost any animals?"

"Not that I know of. I think I'll call around the Hummingbird Falls' Farmers' Association and see if anyone's missing any."

He reached over and removed an envelope tucked under Ellie's windshield wipers.

"What's this? A love note from a new suitor?"

Ellie blushed. "I don't have any suitor, old or new, Mike. I didn't see that before. Please hand it to me."

"Just kidding, Ellie. Don't get so bent out of shape." Mike handed her the envelope with the big block letters on it. "Looks urgent."

"See you later, Mike. Thanks for catching me up on what you've heard. Let me know what you find out from the other farmers. And let's keep in touch. If either of us hears any more shooting, we should call each other and see if we can get an idea of where it's coming from. Maybe we could track it down somehow."

"Will do, Ellie. See you later."

Ellie climbed into her car and Buddy jumped up beside her. She placed the envelope carefully on the seat between them and tried not to read the big letters blaring out to her as she drove toward the library.

READ THIS IMMEDIATELY OR YOU MIGHT BE SORRY.

33

Ellie unlocked the library door and switched on the light. She saw the envelope lying on the floor immediately. Someone must have slid it under the door. She stooped and picked it up. The block letters screamed at her:

OPEN THIS UP OR YOU WILL BE SORRY.

She walked to her desk and turned on the desk light. She looked down at her hands. In one was the note from her car:

READ THIS IMMEDIATELY OR YOU MIGHT BE SORRY.

And in her other hand was the note that warned:

OPEN THIS UP OR YOU WILL BE SORRY.

Somehow the second one seemed scarier.

Ellie sat down at her desk. Buddy stared up at her. "It's okay Buddy. Just some notes. You don't need to worry."

Ellie fished a dog biscuit out of the middle drawer of the desk and handed it to Buddy. He carefully placed the biscuit on his fleece bed and made his ritual round of the three rooms in the library before returning to his bed, lying down and ever so gently picking up the biscuit and nibbling one end.

Ellie opened up the least threatening note, the one that had been under her windshield wipers. It ordered:

GO TO THE LIBRARY AND LOOK AROUND.
ANOTHER CLUE IS THERE TO BE FOUND.
HAWK'S EYES WILL SHOW YOU WHERE TO GO
DO IT FAST AND DON'T BE SLOW.

Ellie sighed. "This riddle isn't too hard, Buddy. I've already found the next note. And I didn't need any hawk's eyes to do it. It was right here in plain view. That's a strange thing to say, 'hawk's eyes.' But then this whole riddle business is strange." She opened the note she found on the library floor.

YOUR NEMESIS IS VERY NEAR
AND IF YOU DON'T SOLVE THE CLUES I FEAR
YOU'LL BE LEFT BEHIND WITH ONLY TEARS.
YOU DIDN'T GO TO CROOKED HEART MY DEAR.
TOO LATE NOW, GO ON FROM HERE
THE NEXT CLUE IS REALLY NEAR AND CLEAR.

How confusing. Ellie looked around. If the next clue was really near, it had to be somewhere in the library. But the riddle didn't seem to give any clues as to where. She didn't see any more envelopes. She looked back at the note. 'NEMESIS' jumped out at her. Who was her nemesis? Why did she have one? What had she ever done to deserve a nemesis? What was she going to do? She would have to call Dave now. This was getting too real, too serious to handle herself. Someone, her nemesis, was after her.

Ellie paused with her hand on the phone. Did she really know what the word nemesis meant? Ellie decided to look the word up in the dictionary, just to be sure before she called Dave.

The definitions ranged from vengeance, opponent and retribution to fate, revenge and doom. Ellie cringed in her chair. Her doom was near. Someone was after retribution. An opponent wanted revenge and to seal her fate. She needed help and now. Oh what had she done to cause someone to stalk her in this way? She couldn't think of anyone, past or present, that she had offended this much. Perhaps the riddler was a psychopath!

She read the note one more time. She noticed that it did seem to offer some salvation. If she followed the clues she wouldn't have tears. Didn't that mean she had a way out? And how did the nemesis know she didn't go to Crooked Heart? Had he been out at Crooked Heart watching for her? Was he following her every step? Was he out there now waiting for her?

She read the note again. The nemesis seemed to forgive her for not going to Crooked Heart. That was a good sign at least. He told her to move on to the next clue. The next clue would be clear.

But where was the next riddle, the one that could clear things up? She thought that was what he meant. Or did he mean that what the clue said was very clear. That could mean her doom would be spelled out in the next riddle. She was in a terrible situation. She had to find the next riddle. Where could it be?

34

Ellie thought about the other notes. The first one she found in an Agatha Christie mystery, *The Pocket Full of Rye*, featuring the wonderful amateur sleuth Miss Marple. Miss Marple was Ellie's favorite sleuth. Ellie let her mind drift. Some of her best ideas found their way to consciousness when she just stopped trying so hard to analyze the evidence. Miss Marple. Such a sweet and treacherously sharp woman. Some of Ellie's friends had joked that she reminded them a little of Miss Marple, especially when she solved the mysteries of Hummingbird Falls last summer. She mused some more, thinking of how she had enjoyed all the Miss Marple books. She recalled *A Murder is Announced* and *The Harlequin Tea Set*. Great mysteries. Another of her favorites was *They Do It With Mirrors*.

Then, "Bingo!" Ellie screamed. She had it. *Nemesis* was the title of another Agatha Christie novel.

"Yes, Buddy, we've got it. It must be Agatha Christie's mystery." Ellie yelled at poor Buddy who hadn't a clue what he had just done to get her so excited. But he followed her to the mystery section of the stacks and waited patiently while she looked through the books on the second shelf.

"Here it is, boy. *Nemesis* by Agatha Christie."

Ellie opened the book and rifled through the pages. Sure enough, right at the page that declared **THE END** she found a folded piece of paper. She put the book back on the shelf and ran to her desk and unfolded the note.

COMING TO THE END
TIME FOR ME TO SEND
YOU TO YOUR JUST REWARD.
TOMMOROW AT 7 P.M.
GET READY FOR HEAVEN
YOU MUST FIGURE OUT WHERE.
YOU MUST BE THERE.

"Oh no. He's coming for me tomorrow. This is just too much. Buddy, you and I are going to see Dave right now."

Ellie put the note into the small cardboard box where she was storing the cup and saucer and the other notes she found. She intended to turn them all over to Dave. He could have them tested and maybe find finger prints that would link the notes to Bamdina or whoever was the author of these threatening riddles. There wasn't much time. Her deadline was 7 tomorrow night. She would just have to close the library. She put the closed sign on the library door. This was an emergency.

Ellie and Buddy raced for the car. She drove to the Town Hall in record time. They scrambled out and pulled open the door to the Police Station. They raced in and then stopped with a lurch.

Ellie screamed. Inside the door stood the man she saw at the fireworks. The man she had identified from the mug books. The man who had been released from prison only a few weeks ago. The man who was allegedly a contract killer. George Bamdina stood in the hallway. He just stood there and stared at her. Had she met her nemesis at last?

35

Dave, Colby and Rosie O'Rourke came running into the hallway, in response to the sound of Ellie screaming. Their hands were on their guns. They stopped when they saw Ellie and Bamdina facing each other. They took wide stances and Dave called, "Freeze. Put your hands over your head and drop to the floor."

Nobody moved. The silence echoed down the hall. Time had ceased for Ellie.

"I mean it. Now. On the floor. Hands over your head."

Ellie grabbed Buddy with one hand, put her other hand over her head and fell to the floor, still holding Buddy, who wiggled and twisted thinking that they were playing a game of wrestling.

Ellie looked up without moving any part of her body except for her eyes. She was the only one on the floor. George Bamdina was standing in exactly the same place he was before Dave issued the command.

"Look, I'm clean." He held up his jacket as he turned around in a circle. "No gun. No hidden weapons. I'm turning around slowly. See? I'm not holding any knives or guns."

Bamdina twirled slowly around. "Look I'm pulling my pants up so you can see. No guns or knives on my legs."

As Bamdina bent over to pull up his pant legs Colby stepped closer and grabbed his arms and twisted them behind his back. Rosie quickly clamped on a pair of handcuffs. Bamdina didn't resist.

"I came here for help," Bamdina said in a calm voice. "I need you to help me. Why are you cuffing me? I haven't done anything."

"An all points bulletin had been issued for your arrest, Mr. Bamdina. You're a suspect in two ongoing investigations at this time," Dave said. "We need to talk to you about your activities and your purpose for being in Hummingbird Falls."

"That can wait. I haven't done anything illegal. I swear. You've got the wrong man. But something is wrong and I need your help."

Dave and Colby frisked Bamdina thoroughly.

"Take him into the interview room and stay with him, Colby. I'll be there in a minute. Be sure to read him his rights. Rosie, you get on the phone to the Greenberg Police Chief. Tell him we've got Bamdina and that he needs to send an officer up here right now to be part of the investigation team. Then call Bill Crandall, up at SBI. Tell him the same. I want him here to handle his end."

"Yes, sir," Rosie said as she ran to the nearest office to use the phone.

Colby led George Bamdina down the hall to the interview room. Bamdina didn't resist but kept repeating that he needed help from the police immediately and that he was innocent of any crimes that might have happened.

Dave looked down at Ellie. "You can get up now, Ellie. I didn't mean you had to hit the floor. I was talking to Bamdina."

Ellie let go of Buddy and stood up, slowly, brushing dirt off her pants. "Your floor needs cleaning, Dave."

"Are you all right, Ellie?"

"No, I'm not all right, Dave. I've just been scared out of my life. I walked in here and saw that man. I thought I was going to die. I thought he would pull out some gangster gun and shoot me. I was so scared. And then you all came running out and I thought I'd be caught in the middle of a gun battle or taken hostage, holed up in the station for days without food or water. Then you commanded me to get on the floor. I didn't hear you identify exactly who was to get on the floor. You didn't say, 'Not you, Ellie, just the bad man had to fall on the floor.' No, what I heard was that if I didn't fall on the floor all hell was going to break loose. I'm not all right, Dave."

"I'm sorry, Ellie. Really. It was an emergency situation that could have easily got out of hand. I needed to take control and fast. You were just in the wrong place at the wrong time. The important thing is we got Bamdina. I'm sorry you were caught in the arrest. Can I get you something to drink?"

"A cup of tea, no make that coffee with milk and sugar. That might help. That's really him, isn't it? I recognized him as soon as I stepped in the door."

"Yes, that's George Bamdina, the one you identified earlier. He must have just walked in here. We'll find out why when we talk to him. How about you have your coffee at my desk and fill out a report for me at the same time?"

"What report?"

"I need two, actually. The first should be your description of what happened, all the details, from when you came in the door to when we took Mr. Bamdina to the interview room. The second report should be you acknowledging that the man you saw here today was indeed the man you saw at the fireworks and found in the mug books. Do you think you could do that for me?"

"I guess so. I need to sit down right now and get my heart calmed down. Maybe a little snack for Buddy and me would help. Then I think I could write the reports. But I came down here to talk to you about something really important Dave."

"Ellie, that's going to have to wait awhile. You can see we have our hands full right now. And we'll have the SBI and Greensberg investigators here soon, too. So, if you could just calm down, take your time, and fill out the reports, I'll talk with you as soon as I can, Okay?"

"I guess it will have to be okay." She and Buddy walked into Dave's office and sat down. "At least I think I'm safe in the Police Station, now that you have Bamdina under lock and key."

Dave followed her. "I'll send Rosie out to get you a turnover or two at the Pastry Shop, Ellie. And some cookies for Buddy, too. Thanks for your help."

Dave turned and left Ellie alone at his desk. Rosie stopped in the doorway a minute later. She handed Ellie two forms and a pen.

"Exciting day, huh? Pretty easy take down. We got him without a shot. Great team work, if I do say so myself."

"I don't know if I'd put it exactly like that," Ellie said.

"Well, here are the reports. They're pretty self explanatory. If you need help just ask me. I'll be right back with your turnovers and coffee."

"Don't forget Buddy's cookies."

"What kind does he prefer?"

"Elizabeth knows, the day old ones usually, no chocolate."

"Got it. Be right back."

Ellie leaned back in the old leather chair. Her heart was still racing and her face felt like it was burning up. When she checked to see if her hands were shaking she noticed that she still had hold of the cardboard box with the notes, cup and saucer in it. She took off the cover to check that the china hadn't been broken by her fall to the floor.

The cup and saucer were fine. Ellie picked up the notes to read one more time before she started to fill out the police forms. She opened the first note. She stared at it in disbelief. Then she opened the second, the third, and the others. They were all the same. She didn't believe it. The writing had disappeared. The pages were blank.

36

Ellie examined the notes again, one by one. She couldn't believe that they were all blank. The ink and writing had disappeared. Now she had no evidence to show Dave. She had told him about the riddles several times, but in each case, Dave was too occupied with other matters to actually look at them. Ellie, in fact, hadn't looked at the notes all together at one time either. She examined each as she found them, worked on solving the riddle and then carefully placed each note in the cardboard box with the cup and saucer. She had no idea how long the writing lasted or when it vanished.

She picked up a magnifying glass sitting on Dave's desk. She held it close to the blank page of one of the notes. She poured over the paper inch by inch.

Suddenly she saw it. One of the letters was very dim, but still readable. An 'A' was barely visible under the magnifying glass. She slowly picked out a few more letters that had not totally disappeared. Then she methodically searched each of the other notes. On each one, some letters were still discernable under the magnifying glass. The other letters were completely gone, invisible.

Ellie took a piece of paper and wrote down the letters that she could find using the magnifying glass from all of the riddles.

mheroooyknWsylynwhhtuoawmLiisPfhiduitpfa7asndalrrifedwlb teoygtioseduodeattCrrpedotalAHnyennetenhiRspirit

"What a jumble of letters. Do they mean something, Buddy? Were they meant to stay visible? Or did they not disappear like the others by some accident, by some mistake the riddle writer made?"

Buddy shook his head. He didn't know either.

Ellie wished she'd copied the notes so she knew exactly what each said. Too few letters remained to help her recall the precise wording, but they did give her some clues. She took some more paper and with the letters she found from each note, tried to recreate the exact wording of each riddle.

She did fairly well, she thought, at least on the first two. After all, she had spent the most time working on them. But the third, fourth, fifth and sixth notes were more muddled, perhaps because they were longer or maybe because she had spent less time working on them. But by the time Rosie returned with the turnover and coffee, Ellie had a pretty good copy of what each note said, plus she had written down the hodgepodge of letters that had not disappeared, in the order she found them.

Rosie put the coffee and turnover on the desk. "What are you working on, Ellie? That looks like a cryptogram."

"Oh, Rosie, you're so smart. You just figured it out. I do believe you could be right. These letters probably form into another riddle or clue. How did you guess?"

Rosie was a little stunned by Ellie's response. "I didn't really guess. I just saw the letters and they reminded me of the daily cryptogram in the paper. I like to fool around trying to figure it out with my morning coffee. They're fun."

"Tell me some tips about solving them."

"Well usually the letters are in groups, like words, so it's easier. You can see the short words and those are usually 'and,' 'the,' 'its,' or simple words like that. Your letters aren't separated so that's going to make it harder. Also, the most commonly used letter is an 'e,' so one way to start is to count up which letter is used the most and call that the 'e'. That is if the letters are supposed to be substituted for others. But maybe this is an anagram and the letters are just scrambled, not coded."

"Oh dear, that sounds complicated and like it could take months to figure out."

"At least there aren't too many letters. That should help. Where did they come from?"

Ellie explained to Rosie about finding the notes and trying to solve the riddles.

"Then when I found that last riddle and it was so scary I became really concerned and knew I had to have Dave's help. I think maybe the riddles are connected with the murder of that woman or that someone's after me for something. I'm scared, Rosie."

"I can understand why. You should've told us right away."

"I tried, but this Bamdina thing came up and Dave just didn't have the time."

"Well, I'll help you look into it. But if you don't mind, could you fill out the report forms first? We need them to process Bamdina."

"Oh yes, of course. I had almost forgotten all about him. What's his story? He said he came to the police station for help. What does he need?"

"He's saying that his wife's missing. Went missing a couple of days ago. He wants to file a missing persons report and have the police start a search."

"Oh my. Do you think that's true? Or is he just trying to distract the investigation into another direction?"

"I'm not sure. He says he was supposed to meet his wife at the fireworks and she never showed up. He was mad at first. He waited another day, but when he didn't hear from her, he decided something must be wrong and came to report her missing."

"So, that could explain why he looked so grumpy when I saw him that night at the fireworks. He was looking all over. I could see his eyes darting, but I thought he looked sinister, when maybe he was just mad that his wife wasn't there when she said she would be."

"That could be. If his story is true and not just a cover up."

"Oh, that's right. He could just be covering up and giving himself an alibi, so to speak."

"Yep. We have to look at what a suspect says from every angle. We know he was at the fireworks because you saw him. He's admitted he was there. Now was he there to meet his wife as he said, or was he there to look around for a child to abduct, or was he establishing some alibi for something else?"

"You mean like for the time that woman was murdered at the State Park?"

"Could be."

"Does he really have a wife?"

"We have verified that he has a wife. He's been married almost eighteen years to the same woman. She evidently waited for him to get out of jail. He says this trip to Hummingbird Falls was purely for pleasure and to get reacquainted after he was released from the penitentiary two weeks ago. This was like a honeymoon trip, he said."

"Like you said, if we can believe him. Maybe he wasn't with his wife. Maybe he was having an affair."

"We're checking that out, now. Dave's questioning him and Agent Crandall will interrogate very vigorously when he arrives. He has files on George Bamdina that expose his whole life. Agent Crandall will be able to catch him if he's lying. Plus, we have pictures being faxed and matched."

"Matched to whom?"

"To the picture Bamdina had in his wallet of his wife. And, to the Medical Examiner to check with the Jane Doe found at the State Park."

"Oh. You mean he could've killed his own wife? Or he killed someone else who wasn't his wife? That is, if he's the murderer. It all seems so confusing. I'm glad Agent Crandall's coming. Dave has only handled two homicides before. The first didn't go so well, but he really nabbed the murderer last year and made up for both sets of victims. When will Crandall be here?"

"Any minute. And I've got to go. I've a lot of follow up to do on what Bamdina is saying right now. I have to get it off the tape and check it out, so I'll be busy. Why don't you write down those visible letters and give me a copy? When I get some down time I'll work with them. I'm pretty good at deciphering codes."

"I'm glad to have all the help I can get, Rosie. Thank you. And I'll fill out these reports right now. Should I stick around after I've done the reports?"

"I don't know. When you're done, leave the reports on the desk and ask Dave if he still wants to talk with you."

"Fine. Good luck with your follow ups."

Rosie left to go back to work and Ellie forced herself to work on the two witness reports. She had just about filled in the final report when Dave burst into the office.

"Ellie, remember you said that you got a description of the man and woman who were in the deli talking about getting rid of someone?"

"Yes, Reggie gave me a description."

"Does it fit Bamdina?"

"Now that you ask, Dave, yes it does. Reggie said he was a tall dark haired man who looked like an outsider. Dressed like a tourist. That fits Bamdina."

"Thanks, Ellie. I just remembered you telling me that when Bamdina said he had been in town for several days and visited the local shops. I'm going to get Reggie down here to eye witness him, too. I may have to call Jean and Alma to do a voice witnessing."

"Does that mean you think Bamdina did get rid of some woman? Do you think Bamdina killed the woman found in the State Park?"

"We're still checking that out. How did Reggie describe the woman?"

"He said she was thin, shoulder length brown hair, dressed like a tourist in a matching work out suit, I think."

Dave nodded. "Ellie, that description just about matches perfectly with the description Bamdina gave of his missing wife. I haven't told him about the woman found in the park, but his description and Reggie's are so close that I'd be willing to bet that the woman he was with in the deli is the same woman who was found murdered at the park. Now, whether it's his wife or not, will have to be determined by the Medical Examiner or by Bamdina identifying the body."

"What if it isn't his wife?"

"Then we're back to square one. An unidentified woman's body and a missing woman who don't match."

"And what if it is his wife?"

"Then, we've solved the missing person case. And we've made some advance in solving the murder. We've identified the body, got her connected to a known felon, know when she was last seen. We've got the husband in custody. It's only a matter of time. Either he did it or he has a good idea who did do it."

"Are you going to tell him about the dead woman?"

"No. Agent Bill Crandall is in charge of that. I hand Bamdina over to him as soon as he gets here. And I can tell you, Ellie, it won't be too soon for me. I hate this case."

"I know what you mean, I think."

"One good thing. We've just about eliminated him from being the one who snatched Carrie. His testimony rings true that he's not into that sort of thing at all. Something from his own history. He had a sister who was abducted and hurt pretty badly. He hates pedophiles and anyone who would hurt a child. I believe him on that."

"That's one good thing in his favor. Wouldn't it be strange if he turned out to be the victim in all this? His wife kidnapped and killed, just as he's starting life out all over again?"

"You know, Ellie, he did say something close to that. He was saying how his wife waited for him all through his prison stay, met him at the gate and welcomed him back. He had promised if she stayed with him he would go straight and he claims he quit the mob and went underground to avoid their payback for his quitting. He complained that now that he was doing well, his wife was missing and it just wasn't fair."

"No, it's not fair, is it, Dave? That old cliché, nobody said life was fair, is so true. Life is just what it is. Usually one problem we've got to get through after another, mixed with as much joy and love we can squeeze in. That's why I keep an umbrella in the car. Because I never know when it will rain."

"You said it, Ellie. I've got to get back now. And I have to get Reggie down here. If you finished those witness reports, you can take off. If I need you I'll call. We're going to be really busy down here, so don't expect to hear from me very soon. Thanks for your help. I have to say, without you we wouldn't be as far as we are. I should get the Village Council to deputize you. Forget the library."

Ellie laughed. "The library's wild enough for me," she said. "You don't know how thrilling it can be. In fact, lately, it's way too wild."

She waved good bye to Rosie on her way out. Buddy was so happy to be out of the Police Station that he romped and peed and pooped all over the Police Station's side yard. Ellie dutifully picked up all his business with one of the plastic bags she carried at all times, just in case.

She and Buddy got into the car. She carefully placed the cardboard box with the notes and cup and saucer on floor in back. She knew she had her work cut out for her. If she remembered correctly, she only had until tomorrow, by 7 p.m., to solve the mystery of the whereabouts of her meeting with the riddle writer.

37

Dave, Colby and Bill Crandall were in the interrogation room with George Bamdina. The tape recorder was running. Empty soda cans, take out coffee containers, candy bar wrappers, and a box that once held a dozen donuts were scattered on the metal table. The air in the room was hot and stale, smelling like sugar glazed work-out sweats.

"Let's go over this one more time," Bill Crandall said.

"I've told you and told you everything I know," Bamdina said. "We have to look for my wife. We're wasting time. I know she's out there somewhere. Maybe she's lost. Instead of sitting here going over the same information, let me do something. I want to look for her."

"Hold on, Bamdina, We are looking for her. Her description has gone out and we're looking. What we need to know is what you did to her."

"What? Can't you get it? I didn't do anything to her. I told you. She never came back from her shopping trip. She was supposed to meet me at the fire works. She never showed up. I haven't seen her since the day before the fireworks, the second of July. We were taking a little time apart."

"Why was that, Bamdina? You had a fight, right? You messed her up?"

"No, it wasn't like that. Yes, we had a fight. But it was resolved. We just decided to take some time to cool down."

"What were you fighting about?"

"I told you. Babs was wonderful the whole time I was in jail. She took care of all my business, paid the rent on our place, and came to see me every time I earned visiting time. She stuck by me through it all.

"I didn't tell her that Sheila was visiting me, too. I really didn't know Sheila very well. She was just the friend of one of the guys I worked with. One day she shows up to visit me. She kept coming back. She'd bring me presents, things to eat, cigarettes, things I needed. She was fun. Told a lot of jokes. Kept me current with what was going on down in the city. I admit I liked seeing her."

"Why didn't you tell your wife that Sheila was visiting you?"

"She's the jealous type. I didn't think she'd understand about Sheila visiting. Sheila's a knockout. She used to dance at strip joints and she's been around. She loves to strut her stuff. You know what I mean? She sticks out in a crowd. The other cons loved it when Sheila visited. She gave them something good to look at. And more. She flirted and fooled around with some of the guys when the guards weren't looking. You know what I'm talking about, don't you? She helped me out of trouble by doing that. If anyone on the cell block started to mess with me then I would threaten to stop the visits from Sheila. The guys that were tight with Sheila backed me up, so I was pretty much left alone so they could get their fix when she came up and played around."

"Okay, so you didn't tell your wife. Then what?"

"Well, after I got out, Sheila wanted to see me. I told her no, that I was with my wife and starting life over again. I quit the mob because I promised my wife I would. I wanted it too. But Sheila kept after me. One day Sheila called me at home and my wife answered the phone. Oh god, there was hell to pay."

"What do you mean?"

"I tried to explain to Babs that Sheila was only a friend. We'd never done anything together, just talked at the jail. Okay, maybe I flirted with her a little, made some promises about when I got out, but I swear, I never touched Sheila. Babs wanted to believe me, but was having a hard time, so I suggested that we get away, come up here to the mountains for a second honeymoon. I hoped she'd forget all about Sheila."

"But she didn't, did she?" asked Crandall.

"I thought so for a few days. Then all of a sudden Babs started up again about Sheila. Wanted me to call her while Babs was listening and tell her to get out of my life once and for all. I agreed. I would have agreed to anything to get Babs off my back and to start making things right again. I told Babs I'd take care of it."

"And did you call Sheila?"

"Yes, Babs listened in on the extension. I thought everything went well. Sheila was really mad, but what the hell? I didn't go after her; she came after me. She still wanted to see me, but I said absolutely not. Sheila said I'd live to regret it and hung up. I thought that was the end of it, but Babs said she needed a day or two to think things over. She went on a shopping trip to the discount stores down in Greenberg. I guess to get a little pay back. She never came back."

"And you, what did you do?" asks Crandall.

"I told you. I played golf, played poker, drank, fell asleep, played golf, played poker, drank and went to the fireworks to meet her. She never showed up."

"You have any witnesses?"

"The three other guys I played golf with. Their wives were hiking some trails in the mountains for a couple of days. We four guys stayed together for two days partying and playing golf and poker. The Inn by the River will tell you about it. They practically threw us out of the place. We were pretty rowdy."

"Anything else you can tell us? Any reason someone would want to hurt your wife or you?"

"Hurt my wife? What? Do you know something? If you do, tell me now."

"Hold on, Bamdina. Hold on. I just asked you if anyone would want to hurt either of you."

"You know, you don't just leave the business. Nobody leaves the business alive. I told them I was taking a leave and would be back. But I don't intend to go back. I'm pretty sure they didn't know I was leaving for good. The only one who knew I was getting out was my wife. Wait. Oh no. I told Sheila on the phone I was out of that life and not coming back. Oh God, Sheila must have told the Boss what I said. She was really furious and told me I'd regret dumping her."

"What would the Boss do? What's his name by the way?"

"You know who he is and you know what happens to anybody who walks out on the business. That's why I told him I just needed a long vacation. He understood that. After being in prison for seven years, you need a break. It was all right with him. If he knew I was quitting he'd put a contract on me."

"What if he wanted you back?"

"Then he'd force me by threatening me or my family."

Bamdina broke down in tears. "He got her, didn't he? My wife. They killed her."

"Yes, George, I think so. We've got a body up at the morgue that we're going to ask you to look at. I think it's your wife. She fits the description and the picture you gave us. She was shot and left at the State Park. I'm sorry."

George Bamdina put his head in his arms and wept. Dave turned the recorder off and Colby stood and leaned against the wall. Bill Crandall moved his chair a little closer to Bamdina's.

"I'm sorry George. If it is her, we'll do all we can to find her killer. Maybe a good revenge would be to help us out with that. Take your time. It isn't easy to lose someone you love."

38

When Ellie and Buddy arrived home there were three messages on the answering machine. The first was from her son, Sandy, wishing her a happy birthday. He apologized because he couldn't remember if her birthday was today or tomorrow. He said he would call back tomorrow just to be sure and that he loved her.

The second call was from her daughter Allison. She, too, wished her mother a happy birthday and sent her love and said a card was in the mail. She acknowledged that she was a day early, but that she was attending a conference tomorrow and didn't know if she'd have a chance to call then.

The third message was from Sarah, saying it was high time for them to have a meeting about the goings on in Hummingbird Falls. She apologized and said she had to renege on her dinner invitation for tonight. Would Ellie meet with her at the Hawks Inn for lunch tomorrow instead so that they can begin to work on the shooting issues and other crises that were endangering Hummingbird Falls. Ellie gave Sarah a quick call and left a message that she would be happy to meet her tomorrow at noon and thanked her for the suggestion.

Ellie had been so wrapped up in the riddles that she completely forgot about her birthday, not that she spent a lot of time musing about her age or about how to celebrate the arrival of a new year in her life. She didn't mind being the age she was now, but didn't much like the reminder that her age was about to change and that she would be even older tomorrow. She was happy her children were thinking of her and remembered her special day. For a moment she missed them so much her heart hurt. Then she was glad that they weren't here to worry over her, her nemesis and his riddles. They would probably insist that she move in with one of them or have a companion who would follow her around every minute, keeping her safe and out of harm's way. Out of life, was the way Ellie saw those suggestions. Besides, she had Buddy as her constant guard and companion already. She intended to be on her own and independent just as long as she was able to. No, she would tell them all about this mystery after it was over. Then they'd all have a good laugh about it.

That is, if everything turned out all right. That is, if she could just solve this last riddle.

She sat down at the kitchen table and took out the paper on which she had copied the letters which had not disappeared. She found some more paper and copied the letters, in a larger size, and then cut each letter out so she could move them around like scrabble pieces. She spread them all out on the table and stared at them. This was going to be a very tough puzzle to figure out. She could see that.

She remembered Rosie's advice and counted the number of each letter, in case the riddle was a cryptogram. There were 11 't's, 9 'e's, 8 'o's, 8 'i's, 7 'r's, 7 'n's, 7 'a's, 6 'd's, 5 's's, 5 'y's, 4 'l's, 3 'u's, 3 'm's, 3 'h's, 3 'w's, 3 'p's, 3 'f's, and 1 'k', 'b', 'g', and '7'.

She tried assigning 'e' for the most common letter, 't', 'a' for the next most used letter, 'e' and so on for the vowels. Then she paused. Where should she go from here? She put off the decision and fixed herself a cup of tea and gave Buddy a biscuit and herself three cookies. Then she went back to working on the puzzle.

Getting nowhere with the cryptogram she switched to the scrabble pieces and started trying to form words. She made the words 'and', 'total', 'terrified', 'sly', 'kill', 'dead', 'trapped', 'snuffed out'.

"These are awful words, Buddy. If they are all like that, then I'm doomed."

Ellie decided that she better stop for a while and calm down. She realized that she was only forming negative words. She needed to try a more optimistic approach. Maybe the message wasn't as bad as she making it.

"I know, Buddy, I'll start again only this time try to find more positive or at least neutral words." She was just beginning again when the phone rang.

"Dave here. Ellie, I thought I'd call you and let you know that George Bamdina's identified a picture of his wife's body. Bill Crandall presented the Medical Examiners' photo to him and Bamdina practically fainted when he saw her. He's very upset and seems sincerely sad about her death."

"Dave, that must help push the investigation forward. So, the unknown corpse was his wife. And it sounds like you don't think he was the killer. Who did kill her then?"

"Bamdina started blaming his old friends and business partners right away. Seems you don't leave the syndicate high and dry like he did. He thought since he had been out of the loop, being in prison, that they would let him go. But I guess they had other ideas."

"So they sent someone after his wife?"

"Looks like it. He thinks Frank Flitio, one of the contract hit men, came into Hummingbird Falls, kidnapped and killed his wife. Seems Flitio is pretty inventive with his kills. Tries to match them to the locale. Like here in Hummingbird Falls he'd most likely choose a shot gun because they are so common here. And he'd stage the death so it could be seen as a hunter's accident, slowing down any investigation into the death. Flitio is probably responsible for the gun shots a lot of people reported. One of them was the killer of Babs Bambina. He might have fired others in pursuit of her or maybe he traveled far away from the vic's body afterwards and shot to distract us from where he killed her."

"He sounds so ruthless and scheming."

"He's a professional. Good at his job. Bamdina thinks Flitio will come after him next. He and Crandall are working out a deal for witness protection if Bamdina agrees to testify against his old syndicate. Right now, he's mad enough about his wife's murder to do it."

"Wow. This investigation's going to spread like maple syrup on a hot pancake. This goes all the way back to New York, then?"

"That's what Bill Crandall thinks. So, we're still running around down here and will be for more hours. I just wanted you to know about the wife."

"Do you think the murderer, that Flitio, is still around Hummingbird Falls, Dave?"

"Don't know, but Bamdina doesn't think so. Flitio kills and leaves. So Bamdina thinks he left the area immediately. Probably would come back if Bamdina stayed, but more likely would knock Bamdina off somewhere else. Contract killers like Flitio like to spread their assassinations out in time and place so there's less chance of a collection of any trace evidence at any one location. That is, unless he can take them out all at one time in one place."

"So we're safe?"

"I think so, Ellie."

"So all the gun shots were from Flitio? Weren't there too many to just attribute them to him?"

"We haven't had a report of any shooting for a day now. I really do think it was mostly kids and fireworks. Maybe someone target practicing. Probably some of the shots were from Flitio trying to set up Bamdina's wife's murder to appear as a hunting accident. Nobody else was hurt that I know of. Nobody has reported any missing pets or found dead carcasses, so there's nothing to go on there. For now, I'm just writing it up as fireworks. I think you should talk with Sarah, who's been causing quite an uproar about the noise, and calm her down. Could you do that for me, Ellie?"

"Sure, Dave. I'm meeting her for lunch tomorrow to talk about all that's going on and I'll tell her what you said. Is the Bamdina business still confidential?"

"Oh, no. That will be in all the papers first thing in the morning. So, feel free to talk about it to whomever you wish, Ellie. After all, you were a central figure in this investigation. I might add, once again."

"Dave, don't remind me. I'm having enough trouble reducing my reputation as a nosy sleuth now."

"It's going to be a long time before anyone in Hummingbird Falls forgets your part in last summer's mysteries. Add this year to it and maybe we'll have to put up a statue of you," Dave laughed.

"No, no, no," Ellie protested. "Let's just work on forgetting it."

"Gotta go, Ellie. I haven't forgotten those riddles you have. Maybe tomorrow I'll have some time to go over them with you."

"Well, we could talk about it then, I hope, but the situation has changed. I won't go into it all now, but if you have a minute you can ask Rosie about it. She's helping me. I only have until 7 tomorrow night. After that I'm afraid it will be too late."

"What do you mean, too late?"

"In the last note, the riddler announced that I have to meet with him by 7 p.m. tomorrow night. But I have to solve the riddle to find out where I'm supposed to meet him. And if I don't solve the puzzle in time to meet him, then he threatened something awful might happen."

"Damn, they've gone too far. Has he told you what he is planning to do at this meeting?"

"Do you think it's more than one person, Dave? The notes seem to be from just one individual as far as I can tell. No reference to being part of a group."

"I have no idea. I don't know why I said 'they'. It just popped out. So did he say what was going to happen at the meeting?"

"No, just something about giving me my just rewards, whatever that means. So, I don't think I want to meet up with him alone. Anything could happen. But I certainly do want to find out who this riddler is and give him a piece of my mind about how he has disrupted my life and find out why he's doing this to me."

"You're right, Ellie. One of us should go with you. You don't have to go alone. You shouldn't have to be so scared. I should have paid more attention to what you've been trying to tell me. Not that I'm convinced this is any more than just a joke. But just to be sure, someone will stop by tomorrow before you leave."

"He didn't say I had to come alone, so maybe you or Colby or Rosie can come with me. I'd feel safer that way. And on the other hand, he hasn't said what will happen if I don't go to the meeting except that I will be very sorry, it will cost me, and so forth. Dave, I'm scared. What should I do? Am I doing the right thing trying to solve this riddle and meeting with him?"

"Ellie, let me think on that for a bit. I'll come up with a plan. First things first. Let's figure out the location of the

147

meeting. I'll put Rosie on that full time. She's quite a gal. I hope we can keep her on permanently. I think between the two of you you'll figure out the riddle. Then, we'll talk about how to go about meeting with this character. How's that for now?"

"Sounds good, Dave. I feel a little better now. I've been really working myself up into a grand seizure of fear, whether I figure out the riddle, meet with him or don't. No way seems better than the other. Thanks for your help."

"Sorry I've been so preoccupied with the Bamdina business and haven't been able to get more involved with what's happening with you, Ellie. But you know how it has been down at the Station. I'll make sure I stay on top of this riddling stuff from now on. But, I really gotta go now, Ellie, lots of business to clean up. I'll be in touch."

Ellie worked on figuring out the letter puzzle through the evening. She and Buddy visited the porch several times just as a warning to any raccoons that might be planning a return visit. They didn't hear any gunshots. Indeed, the night was lovely. The moon glazed the forest with silver and set the shadows deeply under the pines and spruce. All the night sounds sang to Ellie and Buddy as they closed up the house and went to bed.

"Buddy, good night. We'll think about it tomorrow, right? We'll be just like Scarlet O'Hara in *Gone With the Wind*, and deal with it tomorrow."

And cuddled together, the two fell asleep.

39

The next morning, after working feverishly on solving the riddle for several hours, Ellie felt muddled and even more confused. So she decided to work in her gardens and let the riddle go for a while. She'd take it up with Sarah at lunch when her head was clearer.

She was pleased with the way the little starter plants were growing and bent to the task of weeding around the tiny new shoots. She was surprised that so much time had passed when she looked at her watch and saw it was time to clean up and meet Sarah at the Hawks Inn for lunch. She patted Buddy goodbye and locked the door and left.

Sarah was waiting for her, rocking lazily on the big wrap around porch at the front of the old Inn. They hugged hello and then entered the large front lobby, carpeted in deep maroon. Polished pine floors reached around the carpet and led to side rooms and parlors, furnished with comfortable sofas and chairs and plenty of reading material. All the rooms commanded fabulous views of the mountains surrounding the Inn on all sides.

Sarah led the way to the dining room and instructed the attractive hostess that they wanted a table next to the windows. The hostess was wearing a name tag pinned to her sequined top.

"I'm Millie Buckley, your hostess for tonight. Oh sorry, I mean for lunch. I'm on a double shift today, so sometimes I get the meals mixed up. It's still lunch, ladies."

Sarah and Ellie looked at each other. They realized that this was the Millie Buckley who now lived in Ellie's old cottage with her three children and her husband. Ellie decided to be right up front with Millie.

"Nice to meet you Millie. Actually, I heard about you and your family moving to Hummingbird Falls and I've wanted to meet you. I stopped by one day, but no one was there."

"You stopped by? How did you know where we lived?"

"You happen to live in the cottage I rented for ten years. So I knew just where you are."

"How did you stand it for ten years?" Millie gasped. "It's so old fashioned and rustic, not updated at all. There's only one bath and no cable."

"There was only me there for the most part. My kids only stayed the first couple of summers and then were off to wherever young adults go. We loved it there."

"You did? Wow, that's hard to believe. I could sure use some advice from you on how to make that old place work."

"You know, Millie, I'd be glad to help. Maybe I could help you organize things in the cottage. There were some tricks that I used to make more space. And, I planted most of the gardens so I would love to work with you on keeping them up, too."

"That would be wonderful. I've never planted a thing in my life. I don't know anything about plants or trees or even grass. We had people do that sort of stuff when we lived in New York."

"Oh, where in New York?"

Millie collected herself. "Oh, you wouldn't know it. Just a little suburb outside of a city. Ladies, let me seat you and get you a drink."

Millie led Ellie and Sarah to the best table in the dining room. There were only a few other people eating at tables scattered around the huge room. The room looked nearly abandoned.

"We haven't been too busy. Jerry, the manager, said if things don't pick up he might have to cut back on help. That means me. And, my son Matt who's working in the kitchen. My husband, Todd, is the bartender. He would keep his job, thank goodness, because the Inn does have quite a lively crowd in the bar and lounge most nights. Like tonight we have a huge group party to cater for. That kind of event has been keeping us alive so far. Hopefully, the season will improve with all this good weather we've been having.

"What would you like to drink? We have a special on frozen strawberry daiquiris."

"No, no," laughed Sarah. "That's a bit racy for me. I'll have an ice tea please. How about you Ellie?"

"Ice tea for me too, Millie, thank you."

As soon as Millie left to get their drink order, Sarah leaned toward Ellie and whispered, "Would you have guessed it? Here they are, the Buckley's. Now we can tell the crew down at the Pastry Shop all about them."

"Sarah, we hardly know all about them. We can ask a few more questions, but let's be careful, okay? We don't want to seem too nosy, do we?"

Sarah winched. "You got me on that one Ellie. I didn't really say you were nosy, you know, when we were on the phone last time. No one thinks you're nosy, at least not any more than the rest of us. But you keep getting involved in these things that none of the rest of us would even think of."

"You might be right, Sarah. I'm certainly involved in something right now that's driving me crazy and if you don't mind I'd like to get your opinion on it."

"Fine with me. We can talk about the shooting episodes afterwards. I haven't heard any shooting now for two days. Have you heard any?"

"No, and Dave says he is closing the case unless it starts up again. He still believes it's mostly kids with fireworks and maybe a few other things as well that I'll tell you about in a minute. I talked with Mike and he called the members of the Farmers' Association. No one's missing any livestock. No one's seen any evidence of strange people in the woods or wild animals slaughtered. Maybe it's just kids after all."

"I'm willing to let it go, if, that is, there aren't any more gun shots. I still think something more than kids and fireworks caused all that noise. Maybe it's over, whatever it was. Maybe we'll never know. Anyway, tell me what's going on with you."

Ellie told her the story of Jean and Alma, about seeing the scary stranger at the fireworks, the murdered woman and George Bamdina. Sarah's eyes and mouth widened as she listened intently.

"How could you keep all that a secret from me?" she burst out.

"Dave made me. I couldn't tell anyone. You know what he'd do if I told you before I was supposed to. We'd be in deep trouble. He'd never trust me again."

"That's true. I understand Ellie. But I don't know how you kept it quiet. You must have been stuffed full with all that information."

"If I could ever be stuffed full, that is. I had a hard time not telling you, Sarah. I wanted to in the worst way. But if you can believe it, I'm boiling over with something even more troubling now, Sarah. And that's what I want to talk to you about."

Just then, Millie returned with their ice teas. She was a little shaky with the tray and almost lost both glasses several times on her way from the bar to the table.

"I'm pretty new at this hostess stuff," Millie said. "I'm lucky I got this tray to the table. I've been carrying the glasses by hand. I spill less that way, but Jerry told me I'd have to learn to use the tray when business picks up and I might as well start now, so I'm trying."

"Thank you, Millie," said Ellie. "Have you got a minute to talk? I'd love to hear how your kids are making the adjustment to Hummingbird Falls."

Millie looked around. "It's pretty quiet now. We only have one waitress on, so if more people come in, I'll have to help out, but right now everything's pretty much under control."

"So how are your kids doing?" Sarah asked. "And I'm wondering what you're doing about your mail. I'm the Postmistress and would be happy to assign you a mail box. I'm sure the kids would like to hear from their friends back home. You need to come in to the Post Office and file out a form to get a mailbox."

"Oh, the realtor told us about that. We just haven't got around to it yet. So many things are different here. We had our mail delivered to the door in New York. And the trash was picked up and the streets swept. We had city water and sewer. I don't even know what a septic is, let alone how to work the well if it breaks down. There's so much to learn. Sometimes it's just overwhelming.

"The kids are pretty homesick, I think. This move was a big change for them, but I think Missy and Michael, they're my two youngest, seem to be adjusting bit by bit. To tell you the truth, we're having quite a time with Matt, that's our oldest. Teenager. That says it all. He's in some stage or adolescent phase and really resents having to move here.

"Oh, I'm sorry. I'm going on and on and you ladies are probably hungry for lunch. It's just that I haven't talked to another woman since I got here. Do you want to order lunch now?"

"Don't be sorry, please. We have plenty of time. Millie, if you want to, tell us some more about Matt," said Ellie.

"Thanks, talking about it might help a little. Matt had a tight group of friends at home and he misses them a lot. He begged us to let him live with one of his friends in New York. We had to say no to him and I think he's hated us ever since. Todd convinced Jerry to hire him on here as a dishwasher and general kitchen help. We're trying to keep him occupied and out of trouble."

"Trouble? What kind of trouble?" Ellie asked.

Millie looked around to see if anyone was listening. "I probably shouldn't be telling you this, but you seem like such nice women and I do need someone besides my husband to talk about this with. Well, this was what happened. Matt took Todd's shot gun and went off into the woods. We don't really know what he was doing, but we know he was shooting off that gun out there."

Sarah and Ellie looked at each other. Another mystery solved.

Millie continued, "Then he disappeared at the fireworks and never came home until the next day. We've tried to talk to him. We've grounded him. None of it works. He's driving us crazy. When he's home he just stays in his bed and when he's out he disappears in the woods all day. I'm afraid he's pretty depressed. Oh dear, there's a big group at the door. I have to go now."

Millie handed Ellie and Sarah menus. "I have to tell you the specials for today. We have fresh salmon salad with a side order of asparagus on toast, homemade broccoli soup, a ham and turkey club sandwich special and our famous lasagna is a dollar off today. Your waitress is Doris. She'll be right over to take your order."

"We'll need a few minutes to look over the menu, Milly. Thanks. And thank you for confiding in us. I'm so sorry about your son Matt. Perhaps we can talk some more later, after things slow down. I was a school teacher and I know how confusing life can be for young people today."

"Oh thank you. That would be so helpful. I haven't had anyone to talk with for such a long time. Sometimes it gets lonely without a woman friend. I'll stop by your table later."

As Millie moved off to help the new arrivals, Sarah said to Ellie, "The poor thing. In a new place, hasn't even time to set up a mail box and her kids are unhappy. But did you hear that about the gun? I bet Matt's the one who has been doing a lot of the shooting we've heard."

"I think you're right, Sarah. Seems to fit. If he's been running the roads and the woods with a shot gun at all hours, he could be the one. He wouldn't have any way of knowing the laws or the ways we do things in Hummingbird Falls. He doesn't have any friends. I bet he's furious that he's here. He's probably shooting at anything he sees and as a city kid, who knows if he knows how to aim. Maybe his aim is wild. If he came down near to town, he might even have shot the bullets that hit the back of your house."

"He sounds really troubled. Thank goodness the parents found out he had been using the gun. I hope it's under lock and key now. Maybe Matt should go see James Foster as an outpatient. I know James works wonders with kids. Do you think we should suggest that to Millie?"

"Great idea, Sarah. James is so good with kids that are disturbed, traumatized by events outside themselves that they can't control. That certainly seems to fit Matt's situation."

Doris stopped by to take their order. After ordering, Ellie started to tell Sarah about the first riddle she found in the library book. Suddenly she was interrupted by a horrendous crash.

"What's that? It sounds like every dish in the kitchen smashed on the floor."

They heard loud voices coming from the kitchen. Everyone in the dining room stared in the direction of the sounds. Suddenly a young man ran out of the kitchen and through the dining room toward the front lobby of the Inn.

"I don't give a shit about any of you," he yelled. "I'm done. I'm gone."

Tears were streaming down his face as he was pursued by his mother Millie and his father Todd. As Matt escaped through the front door, Ellie and Sarah watched through the window as he ran down the long steep road toward town. Just as the road curved he jumped over a stone wall and headed across the golf course toward the woods. And then he was out of sight.

Millie and Todd came back into the dining room.

"Excuse us for the interruption. Everything's fine. Our kitchen help just got a little frustrated. Don't worry. Your meals will be out very shortly. Our chef has everything under control. Thank you for your patience," Todd announced. Millie wiped at her eyes with a linen napkin.

"Poor things," Sarah whispered to Ellie. "I hope everything is going to be all right with Matt."

"Me, too," said Ellie, thinking that Matt was definitely not all right and hoping that all the Buckley's guns were now locked up securely.

"He needs help and soon."

40

The dining room settled down gradually and the guests returned to eating their interrupted meals. Sarah and Ellie tried to resume their lunch, but were only picking at their food.

"Sarah, I've lost my appetite. I just can't eat another bite."

"Ellie, I've never heard you say such a thing before. You lose your appetite before dessert? Something must really be bothering you. Is it Matt? The Buckley's?"

"No, well yes, that whole scene, meeting Millie, the mystery about where they came from and what they are doing here distracted me. And, Matt's outrageous behavior certainly was enough to take my mind off food. But there's something else, Sarah."

"What? For goodness sakes, tell me. I thought you've been acting strangely lately. What's going on?"

"Something weird. I need your advice."

"Well, go ahead Ellie. Don't keep me hanging here."

"Like I started to tell you, I've received several riddles over the last several days."

"Oh, what fun. Is someone leaving you notes and clues you have to solve?"

Ellie stared at Sarah. "How did you know?"

Sarah glanced out the window and then flicked her eyes back to Ellie. "I didn't know. I just guessed. Isn't that what riddles are all about? Is that what's happening?"

"Yes," Ellie said. "I've received six riddles. I found the first one in the library and solved it on the same day, not knowing whether it was a joke or what."

"And then what?"

"I found another riddle that I couldn't solve. Then I got another one at the fireworks, a fourth on my windshield outside the Pastry Shop and two more at the library."

"Wow, what did they say?"

"That I'd be sorry if I didn't find all the riddles and solve the last one by 7 p.m. tonight."

"Did you solve them all? What's going to happen tonight?"

"I didn't solve them all. That's why I need your help. And tonight I am supposed to meet the riddler somewhere, but I don't know where yet. That's part of the last riddle that I haven't solved. I've tried to talk to Dave several times, but he's been so busy he's basically just pushed my worry aside. I had the feeling he didn't take the whole situation very seriously. But I told him about the last threat and he's promised to get more involved. He's getting back to me today sometime to help me figure out how to handle the meeting and he's got Rosie working on the word puzzle. But I'm afraid someone will get hurt or I could be in trouble, if I can't solve the final riddle in time."

"Well, show the riddle to me. Maybe I can figure it out," said Sarah.

"That's one of the problems. Most of the words on the papers the riddles were printed on just disappeared. The only thing left on each paper is a bunch of letters I can barely see. I've tried to reconstruct the riddles and have a pretty good idea of how they were worded. But recalling the riddles isn't the problem. The real problem is that all I have now are a bunch of letters that are all scrambled up. Somehow I have to figure out how they go together to get the final clue to what's going on. And I only have until tonight!"

"Oh my, are you sure these riddles aren't really just a joke someone's pulling on you? Maybe some kids are fooling around with you."

"I thought so at first. But whoever's creating the riddles and hiding them is so well organized that I don't think kids could be the culprits. And some of the riddles seem linked somehow to everything else that's going on. I'm pretty sure this isn't any joke. Plus, Sarah, I'm spooked. I'm scared. The last riddle says my nemesis is coming."

Sarah laughed. "Sorry, I couldn't help it. You sound so dramatic. Your nemesis. Oh you poor thing. No wonder you're scared. But, I'm sure it's nothing. What have you ever done to get a nemesis after you? Sure, you're nosy and talk quite a bit, but I don't think that threatens anyone enough to want to harm you."

"Thanks for the reassurance, Sarah. And for the characterization as well. I told you you said I was nosy and there it is again."

"I'm sorry, Ellie. Don't get mad. I'm just trying to think of some reason someone would want to tease you along on a riddle trail."

"What did you say? You think someone's just teasing me?"

"I'm sure of it, Ellie. You're making a mountain out of a mole hill, if I do say so myself. This whole riddle thing is most likely the creation of a bunch of people who thought it would be fun to watch you get all involved in solving mysteries. You do enjoy that reputation and everyone gets a kick out of you being our own Miss Marple."

"Funny, you would say that, Sarah. Miss Marple has been at the center of this from the start."

"Oh, don't pay any attention to me, Ellie. What do I know? Let me help you puzzle this out. Then we can decide if it's serious or not and maybe who's responsible. Do you have a copy of the riddles or the remaining letters? I can work on putting them together. I'm very good at Scrabble, as you know."

"At least Rosie took me seriously. She's working with a copy of the letters and trying to unscramble them for me."

"She is? Oh dear."

"Oh dear what?"

"I meant, oh good. Someone else is helping? Did I say 'oh dear'? I must be getting old."

Ellie looked at Sarah closely. "Do you know something about this that I don't?"

"How can you ask me such a thing? Why would I know anything about these riddles? I don't have time to run around hiding secret notes and writing clever riddles for you to solve."

"For a minute there, just the way you said 'clever riddles', I thought maybe you were the one pulling a trick on me," Ellie said as she searched through her purse. "Here, this is a list of the letters that were still visible. I'll copy them for you right now. The more help I get, the better I'll feel. By the way, how do you know they're clever riddles?"

"Oh Ellie, do you suspect me? I'm just a little old postmistress. Silly, of course the person writing the notes would have to be clever to interest you in solving them. And especially to stump you. Whoever wrote them must be very very good at riddles and smart to boot."

Ellie stared at Sarah for a minute and then bent to her task. She handed the list of letters to Sarah and Sarah studied them.

"Interesting. But there must have been more letters than these in six notes. What happened to the rest of the letters?"

"They disappeared. I guess whoever wrote the riddles used a disappearing ink, except for the letters they wanted to save for the final clue."

"I remember when we were kids, we would use lemon juice to write secret notes. We had to hold what appeared to be a blank paper over a candle and then the lemon juice was activated and we could read what the note said. That was a good trick. But how do you make disappearing ink? Now see, would I ask you that if I was the one who was using disappearing ink?" Sarah asked.

"I don't know. Maybe you're trying too hard not to look suspicious. But if you help me solve this thing, then I'll know you're not a part of it. Anyway, I'm going to look up disappearing ink on the internet, but right now I'm more interested in what the letters say when they're put in the right order."

Sarah folded the paper the letters were written on and stuffed it into her purse and took out her wallet. She glanced at her watch.

"My dear, look at the time. I didn't realize it's so late. I have to run. Sorry, I have many errands to complete. But, don't worry. I'll study these letters as soon as I have time. Until then, don't fret so much. I'm sure you are making more out of this than is necessary. Whoever is behind this has no reason to want to harm you or anyone else. It's most likely that someone's playing you and trying to one up you at your own game."

"But you haven't even heard what the messages say," Ellie protested. "How can you be so sure that this is just a game? Sarah, how can you just leave me like this? I counted on you."

"Ellie, I'm not leaving you. I'm going to work very hard on these letters. Right now, though, I have some things I just have to do. With all that went on here today, I'm way behind. Now, just be calm. Don't overreact. I'm sure that we'll find out this is all just one big joke."

"Sarah," Ellie protested. "I only have until tonight."

But Sarah had already left money for her meal on the table, kissed Ellie on the cheek and then scurried quickly across the dining room toward the exit. Ellie sat in shock. How could Sarah treat her this way? Why had Sarah dismissed the riddles as just a joke when she didn't even know what they said?

Millie appeared at Ellie's table. "I'm sorry for all the noise. Your friend Sarah didn't leave because of that, I hope."

"No, she just had to go do errands, I guess. She ran out rather hurriedly, but she left money for her lunch and a tip. If you don't mind I'd like to see the dessert menu. If I have to eat alone, I might as well have something sweet and yummy."

Millie returned with the dessert menu. Ellie looked it over and then said, "I'll have the double chocolate brownie sundae with fudge sauce, whipped cream and nuts."

"Do you want a cherry on top?"

"Why not? One never knows what will happen in the next day, or hour, or minute for that matter. I could be dead tomorrow, so I might just as well enjoy myself right now."

Millie looked at Ellie. "Is something wrong, Ellie? Can I help?"

Ellie looked up at Millie's face. Under the heavy makeup and beneath the bleached blond hair that hung down in her face, was a look of concern.

"You have enough to deal with right now, I think, without adding my concerns. But thank you, Millie, for caring. That's very nice of you."

"Maybe we could get together and talk sometime soon. I could use a good friend and it sounds like you could use someone to talk with too. What are you doing after lunch? I have a break until four. We could take a walk and talk."

Ellie saw the pleading eagerness in Millie's eyes. She was like a puppy beseeching some attention.

"Well, I do have something pretty urgent to take care of, but maybe you can help me with that. Are you any good at word games?"

"Word games? Well, I love to do crossword puzzles. I'm pretty good at that. I could almost always finish the New York Times Sunday Crossword. Will that do?"

"That will do just fine, Millie. Cancel that hot fudge brownie sundae. I'll wait out on the porch for you."

"Great. I'll be there in ten minutes. Thank you."

"Thank you, Millie. I think you may be just what I need right now."

Ellie picked up her things, left money for her meal and a big tip and walked out to the front porch of the inn. She settled in a porch rocker set apart from the cluster of other rockers that decorated the porch and retrieved the paper with the list of letters from her purse.

"I'll figure this out, or die trying," she muttered. Then she put her hand to her mouth. "I better be careful what I say, even if it is only to myself. I don't want to end up riddled to death."

41

Millie walked over to Ellie and sat down. She glanced at the paper Ellie was reading. "Does that have something to do with why you asked me if I like word games?"

"Yes. I'm trying to put these letters into some sensible order. They should spell out a message, I'm assuming."

"Have you figured out the vowels yet? Usually, 'e's and 'a's are the most numerous."

"I think the letter 't' must stand for the 'e' if this is a code. There are more 't's than any other letter. But I've been trying to put the letters in some order using them just as they are, first. Sort of like a word scramble. If that doesn't work, then I guess I have to go the code route."

Millie looked at the letters. If you put one 'I' with those two 'n's you would have the word, 'Inn'."

"Oh great! You're good at this. How did you see that?"

"Maybe because I'm working at an inn and it's been on my mind. I never worked before and never thought I'd be a hostess and serving in an inn in the mountains."

"I can see you have a story to tell, Millie. Let's put these letters aside for a moment. If you don't mind me asking, what was going on with your son? Is he all right? Where did he go? He seemed very upset."

Millie's eyes teared up. "I don't know where he went. He's been disappearing now and then ever since we moved here. He's been acting strange. I don't know what to do. I called his psychologist back home, but he just says to make sure Matt takes his medication and to find another doctor here who can help him. I don't know who to go to or even if Matt would go if I found someone."

"Oh my goodness. That's terrible. Poor Matt and poor you. So, he was troubled before you all moved here? And then the move must have really upset him."

"Believe me, the move upset us all. Maybe more so for Matt. I was hoping being up here would bring us all closer together. Matt has a lot of anger towards his father from way back. I thought one good thing that this move could do is force them back into some kind of father-son relationship. But I'm beginning to think we've made a terrible mistake. Not that it isn't beautiful up here. And everyone's been very nice to us. It's just that it's so different. And we don't know anyone. It's been so lonely. And Matt worries me so much."

Millie burst into tears. Ellie reached out and put her arm around her and offered her a tissue from her purse. She let Millie have her cry for a while and then very gently said, "I think I know someone who can help Matt. He's a very wonderful social worker. He loves kids and has a very respectable reputation. He lives right here in Hummingbird Falls."

Millie dried her eyes and looked at Ellie. "Who is he?"

"His name is James Foster. He's the Director of the Foster Home for Children. He works with kids who have had trauma in their lives, mostly from the loss of their parents, but he's an expert on dealing with loss. And it sounds like Matt's really angry about something, even more than having to move away from his old life. And that's a loss, a really big one, especially for a teenager."

"Do you think he would see Matt?"

"I know James very well and I'm sure he would be interested in talking with Matt. The more important question is will Matt agree to see James Foster?"

"I don't know, but I'm going to do everything I can to convince him. I think if things don't change he could be in real trouble, maybe do something bad to someone else or to himself. I couldn't bear that."

"Millie, I'm seeing James Foster tonight. I'll speak to him about Matt if you want."

"Oh, thank you. Please do. I'd be so grateful."

"There, that's settled. You talk to Matt and I'll talk to James. Now I really do have to get on with this puzzle. I'd love to hear more about what brought you here and how I can help you but right now I have to get these letters to make some sense. I only have until 7 tonight to get this solved. So, if we take Inn as a word, what would go with that?"

They studied the letters together. "Why don't we just play that game where you have a bunch of letters, like these, and you try to make as many words as you can? I'll make a list and you make a list and then we'll compare them and see what we come up with," Millie suggested.

Ellie smiled at Millie. "I can see that we're going to become great friends. What a marvelous idea. Let's do it. Here's a pen and a piece of paper. Let's give ourselves ten minutes and then we'll compare lists. For the first time, I feel like I might have a chance to dig myself out of this confusing mystery."

Ten minutes flew by. Ellie looked at her watch and called, "time."

The two women compared lists.

"Oh my gosh!" gasped Ellie. "I think I know what it says."

42

Matt kept running. He ran until his side ached and he couldn't get enough air to fuel his legs. He finally collapsed on a bed of moss next to a brook in the middle of the forest. He lay still trying to get control of his ragged breaths. When he could breathe again he started to cry.

He didn't mean to cause so much trouble. He didn't plan to shoot the shotgun into the back of some lady's house. He was just fooling around and the gun went off. He must have forgotten to set the safety.

He didn't think he shot anyone in the Park. But he knew he wasn't very accurate with the shotgun. Could he have hit that person who died by the stream? He was shooting around there before the crime scene tape went up. He couldn't bear it if he killed someone.

He was sorry he killed the little birds, crows and squirrels. He was just shooting for fun. The animals looked like targets to him at first. But when he saw their battered bloody bodies, he put the gun away. He hung it up high in a tree so no one would find it. He buried the little birds and squirrels.

He was sad he had been mean to his family. He was so mad at his father for being a crook and humiliating them all. He was furious that he and his brother and sister, and most of all, his mother, had to pay for his father's mistakes. He just couldn't stand what had happened to them.

The worst part was moving away from everything he had ever known. Friends he had since kindergarten. Places he hung out. Things he knew about without thinking. He didn't know anything about the mountains. He didn't know anyone here. He hated everything about coming here. That was why he had to run.

On his first run away down that path behind the house and into the woods he was surprised. The woods were comforting and quiet. He smelled old leaves and new buds. The sight of the azure blue sky through the green leaves awed him. A feeling of peace visited when he just sat alone and shut his eyes.

And then, the dead body. He had seen her before the Park Ranger found her. He had frozen in fear looking down into the dead white face of the woman in the river. He had never seen a dead person before except on TV. He was terrified and didn't know what to do. He was afraid he had killed her. So he ran. He didn't tell anyone what he had seen. He was haunted by the sight and the secret he held.

And his father. He could never talk to his father and his father had never taken the time to try to talk to him. He was always too busy at work, always had too much to do to spend time with his eldest son. Matt believed that his father hated him as much as he hated his father. There was a definite coldness that hung between them. And yet, Matt wanted his father to love him, to be a real father to him. As much as he hid his feelings, Matt loved his father as much as he hated him. It was all too confusing.

The final straw was having to go to work at that lousy inn. He had to clean other people's unwanted food off their plates before rinsing the plates and shoving them into the commercial dishwasher. He had to wear big rubber gloves and stood for hours by steaming dishwashers, emptying garbage into dumpsters, being bossed around by everyone and getting so smelly and dirty, isolated and tired. He just couldn't take it any more. When he dropped the tray of glasses and the chef screamed at him, he ran. And he ran.

And now what? If only he had the shotgun. But his father had taken it and locked all the guns in the trunk of the car. Matt still had his knife, back in the lean-to he built. His Swiss Army knife, a birthday gift from his father, was hidden there. He figured that would do the job.

Matt stopped crying and wiped his nose on his dirty t-shirt. He looked around and headed in the direction of his lean-to. He'd find his knife and then it would be over. He wouldn't have to cry any more.

43

Ellie and Millie stared at the lists they made. Several words appeared on both lists: 7, day, at, be, you, in, on, to, the, all, will, this, for, come, time, Hawks, there, Inn. In addition, each of them had other words written down that could also fit into the puzzle.

"Oh, this's a big help. Let me see. Hawks and Inn go together. Hawks Inn. Right here. This must be where I'm supposed to meet him."

"Him? What's this puzzle all about, Ellie? Is someone playing a game with you?"

"To tell you the truth, I don't know. I've been receiving these riddles for a few days. From the first they were really scary, telling me I'd be sorry, I'd better hurry to meet a deadline, that if I didn't solve the riddles it would cost me. Things like that."

"That's awful. Didn't you go to the police?"

"I tried, but Dave is really busy right now with another case, a big one. Rosie, the new recruit, is helping me. I gave her a copy of the letters and she's working to unscramble them, too.

"Sarah and Dave think it is most likely someone just fooling with me. Why? I haven't a clue. But when the riddler told me my nemesis wanted to meet me, and then the words disappeared, leaving only this scramble of letters, I got scared to death. So, it's important that I solve this as soon as possible."

"That's quite a mystery, Ellie. I hope you can put the words into readable sentences and find out what this person wants from you. I hope I helped a little, but I have to go now.. I don't have much time before I have to go back to work and I want to check up on Matt, see if he went home."

"I understand completely, Millie. I hope he's all right and will listen to you about seeing James Foster. Thanks for all your help and support. I'm going home and finish this riddle up if it kills me."

Ellie walked to her car, her mind working so hard on figuring out the puzzle that she almost missed the piece of paper that sat under her windshield wipers.

"Oh no. Another one."

Ellie took the folded paper and got into her car. She locked her door and looked around. She didn't see anyone but Millie who was driving out of the parking lot in a red Mustang.

She opened the paper. There in the familiar block letters was another riddle:

YOU ARE MAKING PROGRESS PRETTY FAST
YOU'RE NEARLY READY FOR THE BLAST
YOU SEE THE DIE HAS LONG BEEN CAST

YOU UNDERSTAND YOU CANNOT LAST
SO SAY GOODBYE TO ALL THAT'S PAST
AND EVEN AT FIVE TIMES TEN PLUS FOUR
THERE'S MORE.
BETTER SOLVE THE SCRAMBLE AND BE ON TIME
OTHERWISE THERE WILL BE ANOTHER CRIME.

Ellie sighed and folded the paper and put it into her purse. She had been see-sawing for days between thinking these riddles were someone's idea of having fun with her and fearing that the riddles indicated that someone very sick was trying to scare her and possibly hurt or kill her. This last riddle ended with a very frightening word: crime. What crime will happen if she can't solve the whole scramble puzzle before 7 tonight? She flipped back to the belief that the riddler was serious and dangerous. She had better be careful.

She drove off, keeping an eye on her rear view mirror. Nobody seemed to be following her. She'd go home, get Buddy and go right down to the Police Station and see what progress Rosie had made on the word scramble. Then she would insist that Dave do something to protect her.

She turned into her driveway. She had only gone a little way before she saw something lying in the driveway in front of her. She thought it looked like a raccoon at first and wondered if someone drove down here and hit it. As she approached closer she saw it was not a raccoon. It was Buddy.

Buddy was always locked in the house when she couldn't take him with her. What was he doing out here? Who let him out? Why was he just lying there?

She slammed on her brakes and yelled, "No. No. Whoever you are, leave my dog alone. Get me if you want, but don't hurt my Buddy."

Ellie jumped out of the car and ran toward her friend and companion. She kneeled down and patted his head. Her tears blinded her as she bent over her faithful and loving dog.

44

Ellie was crying so hard at first she didn't notice that Buddy was licking the tears off her face.

"Buddy. Buddy. You're alive. Oh, thank you Lord. Now, Buddy, lie right there. Don't move. I'm going to call the vet."

Buddy yawned and wriggled to get free of Ellie's clinging arms. As soon as she moved to get up he sprang to his feet and barked and jumped up on her just as he always did when he first saw her after she had been gone for a while.

"Buddy. You're all right. You aren't hurt? Oh, Buddy, I was so scared."

Ellie started to cry again and hugged Buddy to her as he jumped up. The two stood in an embrace until Buddy struggled free again and ran around in a kind of happy to see you dance.

"How did you get out, you rascal? Did someone break in? Did they let you out? What are you doing here? And, thank goodness you're smart enough to stay on the driveway and not go out on the road. Oh I'm so glad you're not hurt."

Buddy climbed into the car with Ellie and they drove on down to the cabin. The front door was locked, just as Ellie left it. She unlocked the door and let Buddy in. He didn't growl or bark, but she called out anyway.

"Is there anyone here? If you're in there you have a surprise coming. I've called the police and they're on their way."

No sounds came from the inside of the cabin. Ellie could hear Buddy's toe nails clicking on the pine floors as he walked through the rooms. She heard him lapping up water from his water dish in the kitchen. She decided it must be safe, so she slowly walked in the door. She didn't see any signs of an intruder. Everything was in its place. But how did Buddy get out?

Ellie walked through the house to the back screen porch. She had left the door from the house to the screen porch open for Buddy so he could enjoy the fresh air and sunshine that spilled down and heated the flagstone floor. Then she saw it. The screen door to the back yard was open. There was a long rip in the screen. Buddy must have left the porch through the screen door. But did he rip the screen? Or had someone ripped the screen so they could reach in to unlock the door?

Ellie quickly dismissed the idea that Buddy ripped the screen. He had never as much as scratched at the screens on the porch. Even when he heard noises in the woods or the backyard he just barked and ran back and forth across the porch. He had never tried to jump or rip through the screens.

So someone else had been here. What did he want? Was he looking for her? Was it her nemesis growing impatient and wanting to bring things to a close? Whoever it was, he wasn't here now. Ellie walked to the phone and called the Hummingbird Falls Police Station.

45

Millie returned to the Hawks Inn at four. She walked over to the bar and nodded at Todd.

"I need to talk with you."

"I'm busy here. I have people just coming in now after work. I'll talk to you later."

"Todd. It can't wait. I have to talk to you now."

Todd put a draft Miller in front of one of the men sitting at the bar and said, "Everyone all set for now? I've got to take a short break, but I'll be right back."

A couple of the men laughed and one said, "If you gotta go, you've gotta go. Hurry back though, the evening's just beginning."

Todd joined their laughter and then walked back to the room the staff used during breaks.

"What is it, Millie? I can't just leave my job anytime you want to talk."

"Todd, just listen. Matt isn't home. Missy says she hasn't seen him. I drove all over town looking for him. He isn't anywhere. I think he's gone into the woods again."

"So? He's gone there before, Millie. What's the big deal?"

"Todd, he's your son. He's hurting bad. All he's ever wanted is for you to notice him and care about him. Now, he's run off after a big attention getting, upsetting, humiliating event. I want you to go find him and show him that you love him. Talk to him. I've got the name of a social worker here in Hummingbird Falls who works with disturbed kids. I want Matt to see him, to get help from him. He needs us to help him, Todd. Can't you see? We have to help him someway. Otherwise, Matt may do something that we all will regret the rest of our lives."

"What are you talking about, Millie? Of course, I love Matt. He must know that. He's the one who has shut me out, every since he found out about the trouble I got into back in New York. He's gotten worse since we moved here. He won't let me touch him or talk to him. I haven't even seen him. At least at home we used to watch TV together."

"I don't care how it happened. It's happened. He's tuned us out. He's lost and miserable. We're his parents and we owe it to him to help him however we can, no matter what has happened

173

before. Will you look for him? Will you act like, be his father? Do you really care?"

Todd rubbed his hand over his eyes. He looked sick, pale and trembling.

"Of course, I care. I love that kid so much. All I want is for us to be able to be close again, like when he was little. But so much has changed. He must hate me so much for what I did. His father's a crook. His father ruined his life. He probably doesn't ever want to see me again."

"No, Todd. What you don't get is that Matt loves you and wants your love, too. He's just so mixed up right now. You're the one he has to work this out with. You're the only one who can get to him right now. I'll take over the bar. I can do that and hostess too. You go find him. Talk to him. And bring him back here. Not to work. Just so we know he isn't doing anything foolish. I'm afraid for him, Todd. I really am."

Millie moved into the arms of her husband. They stood for a few moments together, gathering strength from each other, the way they use to before all their troubles began. Then Todd let her go.

"I'm going right now. I'll tell Jerry that it's a family emergency and that I'll be back as soon as I can. Don't worry, Millie. I'll find him. I bet he's in that lean-to of his back in the woods. I'll talk to him. I promise."

Todd left the room. Millie dried her tears and walked back to the bar.

"Okay, folks. What'll it be? Who needs a drink?"

46

"**I**s Dave there? Ellie Hastings calling."

"Ellie, it's Rosie. I've got good news for you. I've put a lot of the letters into words that seem to work."

"That's great, Rosie, but I'm calling because I think someone broke into my house while I was out at lunch. Can someone come over?"

"Are you all right, Ellie? Is Buddy hurt? Anything missing?"

"Buddy's fine although he did give me a scare. He was outside. The break in happened through the porch screen door. Why Buddy didn't scare him off, I don't know. But, I'll feel better if someone comes by and checks things out. I received another riddle and the riddler's deadline is coming up in a couple of hours. Frankly, I'm getting pretty nervous."

"Hold on, Ellie. I'll be right up. We've finished all our business with Barndina and he's been turned over to the SBI who will most likely put him in the hands of the FBI within an hour. So, we're freed up. See you in a minute or two, make that five. I know Dave is planning on seeing you in a little while too."

Ellie sat down at the kitchen table and pulled the latest riddle out of her purse and read it again. She would show it to Rosie. She looked closely at the print. Was it disappearing as she watched? She quickly copied it word for word in case the ink disappeared before Rosie arrived. And what if some new letters were left visible like in the other riddles? Should the additional letters be added to the others? Or would they form a new message of their own? Would that change the message that Rosie had figured out?

Ellie placed the list of words that she and Millie made out of the scrambled letters on the table, too. While she was waiting she'd try to put the words in some order. She absently munched on a sugar cookie while she moved the words around in her head.

That method proved too difficult. Ellie took her kitchen scissors and cut out all the words. That way she could slide the words around. That was a more efficient way, she determined.

She placed the word 'come' before 'to'. 'Come to'. Then she put 'Hawks Inn' after 'to'. 'Come to Hawks Inn'. She slid the '7' and 'p.m.' together and placed them after 'Inn'. 'Come to Hawks Inn 7 p.m.'

There. She had part of it. The when and where. She knew she had to meet the riddler at the Hawks Inn at 7 p.m. tonight. Now what did all those other letters spell out? How did the other words she had figured out fit together? And were they the right words? She was sliding words and letters around when she heard a car pulling up her driveway. She went to the door and saw the big black Hummingbird Falls' Police SUV stop. Both front doors opened and Colby jumped out of the passenger side and Rosie exited the driver's side. They smiled at each other and walked to the door.

"Hi Ellie. We got here as fast as we could. You okay?" Colby asked.

"Yes, I'm fine. But my screen door took a bashing. Come in and look at it."

Colby held the door for Rosie. She smiled at him. He smiled back. Together they walked through the house to the back door that led to the screen porch.

"I leave the back door open for Buddy so he can go on the porch if he wants to. But I always leave the back screen door locked. I've been especially careful about locking it after my marauding raccoon adventure. Look at it. It's ripped to shreds. It was wide open when I got here. I closed it."

"I brought the finger print kit. I was hoping to lift some prints. But if you touched the door, we might not be able to get clean ones. I'll dust this inside door as well. If the person bothered to break into the porch, it makes sense that he would have come into the house too. Is anything missing?" Colby asked.

"No. I don't think he took anything. Everything was just as I left it."

"I'm going to look around outside," Rosie said. "I'll go out the front door and walk down to the back. Maybe there'll be some foot prints we can make plaster casts of."

While Colby was powdering for prints Ellie moved closer to him.

"What are all the smiles going on between you and Rosie, Colby? Is this another one of your conquests? I thought you didn't like female officers, especially good looking ones."

Colby blushed. "Come on, Ellie. Back off. I'm just getting to know Rosie. She's really nice, easy to talk to. She's been a great help to Dave and me during this Bamdina case. Gosh, every time we needed something, she came through. She's smart as a whip and knows all the new techno and forensic stuff. Plus, she majored in psychology and has great instincts on how to interrogate a suspect. You should have heard her soften up Bamdina. Even Bill Crandall was impressed."

"Sounds like she might be around for a while then."

"Yes, Dave's put in for a new hire. I really hope it goes through. We can use someone with her talents."

"And what talents are those, Colby?" Ellie teased.

"Oh go on, Ellie. I've just met her. I like her. Let's just leave it there for now, okay? But you'll be one of the first to know if something develops."

"Of course, I will. They don't call me the snoop for nothing."

Colby laughed. Rosie called to them from outside the back porch.

"You two better come out here. We've got evidence. Bring the camera, Colby. We need shots of these prints. Walk around from the front and don't let Buddy out."

Colby and Ellie joined Rosie. "See here. And here. There's another one over there."

Colby bent over and examined the prints. Ellie looked, but didn't see any marks of boots or shoes.

"Where are they?"

Colby was still bent over. Ellie could hear a strange noise coming from him.

"Are you choking, Colby? What is it? Why, you're laughing."

Colby stood up and burst out with a howling laugh. "Sorry, Ellie. I can't help it. Really, I can't."

"What? What?" Ellie turned to Rosie who was now laughing out loud too.

"Look here, Ellie," Rosie said as she pointed at a small circle with five little points at its edge indented into the dirt.

"That doesn't look like a foot print," Ellie started to say. Then she took in a big breath and started to laugh as well. "Those little rascals. They came back in the daylight. Would you believe it?"

"They must have come up to the door, found it locked and ripped the screen to get in. I guess Buddy heard them, pushed at the door until it opened and then chased them away. The raccoons never got in or we'd have seen a mess in there," Rosie added.

"Well, I hope Buddy scared them off for good. Two frights from those critters is just about enough. I've got too many other things on my mind now to have to deal with thieving and mischief making raccoons."

Rosie and Colby looked at each other. "Yes, Rosie told me all about the notes, the riddles, the warnings you've received," Colby said. "I was over at Rosie's last night and we worked on the scrambled letters together."

"Oh," Ellie said. "I guess two heads are better than one."

Both Colby and Rosie blushed this time. "Anyway, we made good headway. Let's go in and see what you have and put it together with what we've come up with."

All three worked around the kitchen table, drinking tea and eating cookies and having a rather nice time putting the letters into words and the words into sentences. They finally leaned back.

"I think this could be it, Ellie. There it is," said Rosie.

On the paper in front of them, spelled out in block letters was the solved riddle.

COME TO A PARTY FOR YOU AT 7 P.M. AT THE HAWKS INN ON WEDNESDAY. ALL YOUR RIDDLING FRIENDS WILL BE THERE. P.S. HOPE YOU FIGURED THIS OUT IN TIME.

"Oh my gosh. I can't believe this. You mean all these riddles are about getting me to go to a party? They put me through all this just for a party? I'm going to kill them all. Who all is in on this? Do you two know?"

"Honestly, Ellie. We've had nothing to do with the riddles or what they said. We were just told that it was a fun way to get you to a surprise party. They knew trying to throw a regular surprise party would never work because some how or another you would either suspect or figure it out and then the party wouldn't be a surprise. This way they figured you'd be too busy and distracted to think it might be all about a party for you. All they told us is there was no reason for us to worry if you caused a fuss. That's why Dave kept putting you off."

"But why did you offer to help with the cryptogram then, Rosie?"

"They got worried that you might not solve the riddles in time. When you got all worked up, they wanted to make sure that you weren't too scared to continue working on the riddles. They gave me a copy of the message so I could kind of strategically help you along."

"Well, I guess I'm the laughing stock of the whole town by now."

"Oh no. Quite the opposite. Everyone's amazed you solved so many of the riddles so fast."

"Just who is everyone? Who thought this up? Who planted all the notes? Who wrote the riddles?"

"John, Sarah, Mary, Margaret, Bonnie, Debbie, Larry, Mike and quite a few others really had to work hard to keep you guessing. It took them hours to create riddles difficult enough to keep you challenged," said Colby.

"Well, I'll be. I never guessed that's what was going on. I was convinced that some one was after me, although for the life of me I couldn't figure out why. Although now that I think about it, Sarah acted downright disinterested and uncooperative when I asked her for help. I bet she was right in the middle of the whole thing.

"Who put the notes in the library and on my car and by the T?"

"I'm not sure, but I think they all took turns. The village's been in a whirling buzz for weeks now. Didn't you notice that everyone got quiet every time you came into the pastry shop?" Colby asked.

"No. I guess I'm not as observant as I thought I was. Wait 'til I see them. I'm just going to kill them."

Ellie thought for a minute. "Why did they make it so weird and scary? I was really beginning to think someone might kill me. That wasn't too much fun."

"I agree and so does Dave. Dave was so mad when he found out what some of the riddles actually threatened. He called Sarah and read her the riot act. Told her to lay off with the threats or he would tell you the truth. But by that time you had already found all the riddles."

"I guess they didn't realize that I'm not as brave as I sometimes pretend to be."

Actually, Ellie was starting to feel a little touched about what had happened. In fact, she was feeling very good. Loved even. The whole village had conspired to play with her, to entertain her, to get her to a party.

"Gads. Look at the time. I have to take a shower and get dressed. James is picking me up at 6:00. Thanks for helping me out with the riddles so I can make my party on time. And now I can go to meet with those riddlers without fearing for my death. But maybe they better fear for theirs. I am really going to give them a hard time. I hope to see you both there later."

"We'll be there. Believe me, the whole village will be there."

Colby and Rosie hugged Ellie and walked out to the SUV. Ellie waved them goodbye and stood watching them drive away. She was in shock.

"Imagine Buddy. Everyone was plotting and scheming for us. They sure went to a lot of trouble. But, you know, it was fun, too. At least when I wasn't so scared. Come on, I think I'll give you a bath, too. You can wear your very best bandana tonight."

47

Todd walked quietly down the trail until he saw the rough little lean-to that Matt had built. He stopped and listened. He didn't hear anything. He didn't want to startle Matt and give him a chance to run again. Todd was worried that if Matt ran again, they would never be able to find him. Todd continued to walk until he was alongside the lean-to, close enough to catch hold of Matt if he tried to run away.

He called softly, "Mattie, are you there? It's Dad. I want to talk to you."

"Go away. Leave me alone. I don't want to talk to you now or ever again."

"Matt, please. I need to talk with you. I want to tell you how sorry I am about what happened today."

"Forget it. Today was nothing. Today was everyday of my life, Dad. You don't understand."

"Matt, I want to understand."

"Oh sure. I believe that. You just want me to go back to work so we can have more money."

"Matt, no. That's not what I want to talk about. You don't have to go back to work if you don't want to. Your Mom and I just thought working might give you something to do, or that you might meet someone from the village that way."

"Yeah Dad, tell me another one. You know, you're not such a credible character any more. You're an expert liar. Look at where that got us."

"I'm sorry about that too, son. It's all my fault. I've hurt you all so much, disrupted your lives. If I could do it all over again, believe me, I'd change things."

"Yeah? What would you change?"

"I'd change the ways things are with us, Mattie." Todd said softly.

Matt didn't answer.

Todd continued. "I want so much for us to feel good with each other. To spend time together, to talk. I remember when you were little you'd climb up in my lap and say 'talk daddy, talk'."

"That was twelve years ago, Dad. You haven't talked to me since then, even when I used to beg you to pay attention to me."

"I'm so sorry, Matt. I want us to start over. I want us all to heal from all the hurt I've caused this family." Todd paused. "Hey, do you mind if I come in there and sit with you?"

"Do what you want. You always do anyway."

Todd stifled a reply and walked into the lean-to and sat down on the ground. He looked over at Matt. What he saw shocked him and scared him to his soul.

Matt was lying on a blanket and holding a Swiss Army knife. His wrists were cut and bleeding. Blood had soaked into his dirty shirt. His skin glistened with sweat and he was pale and breathing heavily.

"Matt, what have you done? Oh no. What did you do? Oh God. Let me help you."

"Stay away. I have the knife and I'll stab you if you try to come near me."

"Matt, listen to me. I can carry you out of here and get help. It doesn't have to be this way. Your mom found a nice man in town who works with kids. He's supposed to be really great. We can talk to him. You can talk with him. Whatever way you want it. He can help you, me, and us. We can make it better. I know we can, Matt. I love you. I couldn't go on if anything happened to you. It's all my fault. Oh please, Mattie. Let me help you."

Matt started to cry. He let the knife fall from his hand. His father crept over and took the knife, closed it and slipped it into his pocket. He carefully raised Matt's wrists and examined them. They weren't bleeding very much now and Todd thought that Matt's attempt to slice his wrists missed the main vein. Todd removed his own t shirt and ripped it into pieces. He wrapped Matt's wrists gently. When he finished he put his arms around his son and rocked him. Todd remembered a piece of the song that Mattie loved him to sing when his father put him to bed when he was little. Todd hummed the first lines, trying to remember the words. The last lines came to him and he sang softly, "Sleep now, sleep in peace, Angels will keep you, all through the night."

48

Ellie got dressed in her best clothes. For her that meant she wore her black leather oxfords instead of the Wellingtons, a pair of soft cotton black pants instead of her jeans, and a green silk blouse replaced her flannel shirt. She even put on a lacy bra, although she wasn't quite sure why. She completed her attire with earrings, a silver pin of her mother's and a little eyeliner, blush, lipstick, and a splash of lilac cologne.

"Well Buddy. What do you think? I haven't dressed up for the longest time. Do you think I look good?"

Buddy looked like he wanted to answer her and whined a little bit. Then he tipped his head and thumped his tail vigorously against the floor. He got up and did his little happy dance and barked once.

"I guess you approve. Thank you very much. And now for you. You smell so clean and sweet after your bath. I have just the scarf for around your neck."

Ellie searched through several drawers until she found what she was looking for. "This will do it," she said, pulling out a gold and silver striped tie.

She wrapped the tie around Buddy's neck, knotted it loosely and let the ends hang down a little. Buddy shook his head a bit, but over all seemed quite pleased to be dressed up, too.

Just then there was a knock at the front door.

"James is here, Buddy. Let's be on our best behavior, pal."

Ellie opened the door. James Foster stood there smiling and holding a big bouquet of mixed spring flowers. He looked fine. A blue sports jacket brought out the blue of his eyes and his yellow shirt accented his tanned face. Gray trousers and black shoes completed his casual but very impressive look.

"Why you look mighty handsome, James."

She smiled right back at him. She loved the way his face crinkled when he smiled. His high cheek bones caught the light of the setting sun and gave him a warm, ruddy outdoor good-looking gleam.

"Thank you pretty lady. You look pretty ravishing yourself. Here, these flowers are for you."

"Thank you, James. They're beautiful. Come in while I put them in some water. What's the occasion? Or do you buy flowers for every lady you take out to dinner?"

"Your birthday, of course, Ellie. Happy Birthday."

"Oh so it is. I'd completely forgotten that it was my birthday with all that's been going on. But how did you know it was my birthday today?"

"Well, I don't think I'd be giving away any secrets if I tell you that everybody in town knows it's your birthday, Ellie. Haven't you got that clue yet?"

"That's all I've been getting, James. Clues and puzzles and riddles and scrambled words. What do you mean? What clue am I supposed to be getting?" She had artfully arranged the bouquet of flowers and set the vase in the center of the table.

"Well, if you don't know now, I'm not going to tell you. I have reservations for 7, so maybe we should get going."

"James, I have two things I have to deal with before we can go eat. The first is pretty straight forward. So, I'll start there. There's a boy who needs your help. I talked with his mother today and she's very worried about him. I said I would talk with you and ask if you would see him as a client."

"Most of our kids are residents, you know. But we've been discussing extending our outpatient services. Is he under 18? That's our cut off age."

"Yes, he meets that criterion. He seems so angry and hopeless, at least that's how his mother, Millie Buckley, described him. Can you help him?"

"I can try. The Buckley's, that's the new family in town, isn't it? I haven't met them formally yet. Have them give me a call tomorrow and I'll make sure my schedule has room for them."

"Thanks so much James. My heart just went out to Millie. I know you'll be able to help them."

"What's the other thing?"

"It's a long story and I'll tell you about it after we get there. The short story is that I finally figured out the last riddle."

"Riddle?" James asked.

"I can't go into to it all right now. What's important is that I have to go to the Hawks Inn and meet some people at 7 p.m. Would that be all right with you?"

"Matter of fact, that would be fine. That's where I made our reservations for tonight."

Ellie looked at James. "Are you in on this thing, too? Is that why you asked me out for dinner tonight?"

"Well, yes and no. I guess I better come clean. I'm the one designated to get you to the Hawks Inn. I'm also the back up plan in case you didn't solve the scrambled word puzzle. But I heard Rosie and Colby did a good job of helping you with that, so I didn't really have to be here to take you over there after all."

"Oh, I feel so embarrassed. Here everyone, even you, has set me up. And I didn't even suspect what it was all about. How could I be so dumb? And you got dragged into taking me to dinner as a back up plan because I might be too numb to figure out the last riddle. That doesn't make me feel too good."

"Wait a minute, Ellie. The no part I was just getting to is I've wanted to take you out for a romantic dinner for a long time. And even if this whole scheme hadn't been developed, I was planning to ask you out for a special date. It just so happened that your birthday and a few dozen of your friends got involved with it too."

"A few dozen?" Ellie gasped. "What is this? A town meeting?"

"Maybe not the whole town, but too many to make this just you and me. So I think I'm going to ask you for a rain check for our romantic dinner. What do you think?"

"I'm just overwhelmed with all this, James. But I would love to have a quiet dinner with you when everything finally settles down. Thanks for asking."

Ellie reached up and kissed James on the cheek and he gave her a gentle hug.

"I like this, but we really do have to get going now," James said.

When James drove up to the front of the Hawks Inn Ellie was amazed to see the front porch covered with bright Christmas lights, multicolored crepe paper and balloons. Gathered on the porch were almost one hundred people, friends she had met over the last ten years, acquaintances from her library work, residents she had met at fairs, farmer's markets and festivals and the Pastry Shop.

They cheered as she climbed out of the car and sang a rousing version of Happy Birthday as they escorted her into the large dining room of the Inn. The dining room had been rearranged with a large banquet buffet table on one side of the room, heavily laden with aroma producing foods of all kinds. The tables were decorated with flowers, balloons and champagne glasses.

Ellie saw Millie, in a tight gold sequined dress, standing to one side with Todd. Todd had one arm around his eldest son Matt and the other wrapped around Missy and Michael who were dressed in high New York style also.

Millie smiled and waved at her. Sarah rushed forward and hugged Ellie.

"I'm so sorry, Ellie. I thought this riddle thing up to surprise you on your birthday. I figured you would have fun and it all started just fine. But I didn't know you would get worried and scared. And, I didn't know that a woman would get killed at Crooked Heart, in the exact spot I was telling you to go. So it's lucky you didn't know where Crooked Heart was. I don't know when she was killed, but wouldn't it have been awful if you did puzzle out where Crooked Heart was and showed up there at the same time she did?"

"Maybe more than awful, Sarah. That riddle could have led me to my death, even though you couldn't have known that. So, Sarah. You're telling me this was all your idea? You're the responsible one?"

"Yes, at first. But I can't take all the credit for it. As soon as I mentioned it at the Pastry Shop, everyone wanted in on it. We had so many meetings. Everyone worked on the riddles. Some people had to trail you to make sure you were going to the right places. Others slipped the notes under the door of the library or in library books or on your car. Others kept watch or distracted you to make sure you didn't catch them at it. Whew. We had a time. Actually, I think we all had great fun."

"Not everyone had a great time. Remember me? I had a trying time. And I do hold you responsible, along with everyone else who participated."

"Oh Ellie. You aren't upset with us, are you?"

"Now that it's all over and after I have time to think about it some more, I'm sure that I'll come to believe it was the most clever, adventurous, intelligent, fun, challenging game I've ever played. But right now, I don't know whether I should ever speak to any of you again for pulling this dastardly trick. I was ready to kill you all on sight."

Mike jumped in. "But Ellie, we all knew you were the sleuth. You're the one who loves mysteries and solves impossible puzzles. So we thought you would love this."

"Maybe I would have loved it better if I didn't get so scared."

"Well, it could be we went a little over the top. We tried to make the riddles with double meanings. You could take them seriously, or read them another way," said Bonnie who was listening to the conversation.

"How do you read 'you'll be sorry?' in another way?" asked Ellie.

John Stapes, editor of the Hummingbird Falls Newspaper, chimed in.

"Wouldn't you be sorry if you missed this wonderful party? That was what we meant."

"Well, what's the other meaning of meeting my nemesis, the die is cast, and there will be a crime? That last one really scared me."

"That riddle was just cluing you about your birthday. Of course, your past year is gone and it would be a crime if you missed your birthday party, so to speak," said Margaret. "I wrote that one myself. I rather liked it. Especially the clue that said 'five time ten plus four. That's how old you are today. Didn't you figure that clue out?"

She tossed her inky black hair back over her shoulder and moved toward the bar to get a drink. She looked marvelous as usual, with her floor length pink peony colored Japanese silk Kimono arranged saucily around her near perfect figure. Hummingbird Falls was lucky to have such an eccentric and attractive art gallery owner.

Someone handed Ellie a glass of champagne and Chuck, the minister at the Little Church toasted her with many humorous and complimentary words. Others mingled, laughing and having a good time. The food was being consumed, drinks were flowing, and the mood was light and happy. Hummingbird Falls had come together to celebrate one of its own.

Ellie stood back, enjoying a break from the constant stream of well wishers and tale tellers. She had heard the whole story now and from many different perspectives. Every clue had been explained again and again, whether she had figured it out herself successfully or not. Every step or misstep she had taken on the riddle journey had been relayed to her in detail. She was beginning to understand how much fun the villagers had putting this whole adventure together and carrying it out.

Her crankiness had disappeared like the letters on the notes. She felt she had given the riddlers a hard enough time and was content to stop haranguing them and enjoy them as she usually did. She wished she could have been on both sides, having the fun of devising the riddling game and laughing while she watched herself stumble around trying to figure it all out as well as being the one so loved and cared about who was provided all the riddles to solve.

Ellie sipped her champagne and looked around the room which was filled with close friends, acquaintances, neighbors and residents of her chosen community. She saw James Foster talking with Todd and Matt at one table. Her heart stirred as she saw Matt tentatively return James' smile. Millie was helping out with the buffet and was laughing and interacting with the townspeople. Missy and Michael were talking to some of Jean and Alma's kids in the corner. The Buckley's looked like they would soon have friends and fit in to life in Hummingbird Falls just fine.

Dave walked over to her. "You understand now, I hope, why I didn't jump right in to help you out with those riddles. I hated to see you worry, but I know you well enough to know that you'd figure it out and be okay. I did give Sarah a piece of my mind when I found out how those riddles were worded. Believe me. If I had known what they said, I would have stopped the whole thing. Forgive me?"

"I guess you owed me a few, for the times I've messed things up for you Dave. Thanks for being a part of this. It's very special to me."

"Also I wanted to let you know that Bamdina was safely in the hands of the FBI. He has agreed to testify against the syndicate he was involved with and then he'll start a new life in the witness protection program. I'm sorry he lost his wife when he was trying to go straight, but a lot of good will come out of closing down the drug trafficking his mob's involved with."

Ellie nodded. For once, she had no words to explain about the irony of life.

"The Greensberg Police caught that child molester last night. He attempted another abduction and got caught. He'd been under surveillance since the fourth of July and he finally tried it again and we nabbed him. He's got a felony list a mile long. I don't know why they let these guys out of prison. By the way, he admitted to taking Carrie. He said he didn't do anything to her and decided it was too risky to try to take her away with all the people around and her fighting him so hard. Anyway, they'll send him back to prison for a long time. So, that's one person we don't have to worry about anymore."

"Thanks to you, Dave, Hummingbird Falls is all in order again. Just the way I like it."

"I don't know if it's all in order, Ellie. Have you noticed those two?"

Dave pointed to Colby and Rosie who were sitting alone at a table near the back of the dining room.

"I could swear they're holding hands. And on duty, too," Dave laughed.

"Well, well, well. I'll have to keep my eyes on them," Ellie said. "A new romance in town will give everyone something else besides me to talk about at the Pastry Shop."

Dave's wife Mary walked over with James Foster. "Time for you to cut the birthday cake, Ellie. I made it myself. Seven layer fudge cake with mocha frosting. Hidden inside are little tokens. If you get one in your piece of cake, you'll enjoy what the token symbolizes."

"I hope there are no jokers in there. I don't think I could stand another round of being riddled," Ellie said.

Everyone gathered around the cake as Ellie made her wish and blew out the fifty four candles. Then to a rousing round of Happy Birthday singing she cut into the cake and started serving pieces to her companions. With her head bent over the cake, not many saw the tears well in her eyes.

But Buddy saw them and edged closer to Ellie and licked her hand. He knew these were tears of joy and belonging and he settled down at her feet, waiting for cake crumbs to fall and content to be part of the Hummingbird Falls' family.

When Ellie bit into her slice of birthday cake, her tooth hit on a piece of metal. She pulled the charm out of her mouth and looked at it. What she saw was a tiny replica of an airplane.

"Oh dear, what does this mean?" Ellie asked those gathered around her.

In unison several voices cried out, "You're going on a trip."

"Not me," Ellie said. "I like it right here too much."

Little did she know that the small silver airplane charm that made its way from the cake to her was foretelling her next great mystery adventure.

THE END

JOANNE CLAREY